The

Places

where

Names
VANISH

The
Places
where
Names
VANISH

Stephen
Henighan

THISTLEDOWN PRESS LTD.

Canadian Cataloguing in Publication Data
Henighan, Stephen, 1960 –

The places where names vanish
ISBN 1-895449-77-4

I. Title.
PS8565.E5818 P5 1998   C813'.54   C98-920057-4
PR9199.3.H4515 P5 1998

Book and cover design by J. Forrie
Set in 11 pt. New Baskerville
by Thistledown Press Ltd.
Cover painting by Gustavo Rojas
Author photo by Diana MacDonald

Printed and bound in Canada by
Veilleux Impression à Demande
Boucherville, Quebec

Thistledown Press Ltd.
633 Main Street
Saskatoon, Saskatchewan
S7H 0J8

Saskatchewan
Arts Board

THE CANADA COUNCIL | LE CONSEIL DES ARTS
FOR THE ARTS | DU CANADA
SINCE 1957 | DEPUIS 1957

Thistledown Press gratefully acknowledges the financial assistance of
the Canada Council for the Arts, the Saskatchewan Arts Board, and the
Government of Canada through the Book Publishing Industry
Development Program for its publishing program.

ACKNOWLEDGEMENTS

I would like to thank Brian Bartlett, Laurel Boone, Michael Carroll, Diana MacDonald and Nino Ricci for their useful comments on various drafts of this book. I am grateful to my editor, Seán Virgo, for once again contributing the clear, strong light of his insight and encouragement. I thank Patrick O'Rourke for his continued support of my writing.

— *S.H.*

Como llovizna sobre brasas
dentro de mí los pasos pasan
hacia lugares que se vuelven aire.
Nombres: en una pausa
desaparecen, entre dos palabras.

Like drizzle on embers
inside me footsteps step
towards places turning to air.
Names: in a pause
they vanish, between two words.

— *Octavio Paz:*
   "Pasado en claro"

Part One

❡

ONE ɡ

Footprints.

Squatting in the doorway, Marta watches her mother stroll down to the river past other women's anger. Her long body, the neck as supple and strong as a third arm, holds her laundry basket balanced on her head. Neighbour women too chunky and short limbed to carry their baskets this way swear in envy at the village's black women. They taunt Marta's mother the most. Caught up in the rhythm of their curses, Marta gets to her feet. The glaring dust-drenched air dries her throat. —*Negrita, negrita,* Marta murmurs.

—Come back inside, her grandmother says, taking her by the arm. She leads her into the dim outer room. —The only thing your mami has that those women envy is my son.—

Marta's father, Ignacio, keeps the only shop among the knot of houses drawn tight around the muddy river. During the rainy season white fog drags the cold down from the *páramo*, blotting out the canyon walls. Her father is a hard-working man, but her grandmother claims that his faith in God is deficient. Why else would he have married her mother? No other child in the village has a *mestizo* father and a black mother. In the larger, chillier villages up on the *páramo* there are only morose Indians, a few mixed-blood middlemen like her father and the decent people who own the land and live most of the year in Quito.

—Quito is where rich people live, her grandmother says, picking lice from Marta's hair. —It's like Heaven, except that God is absent.—

No one knows how the village came to have black people. Her grandmother mutters that God visited black people upon them as a curse.

—Juana, the old woman says, is a witch. She cast a spell on Ignacio so that she could become your mother.—

Ignacio had been going to marry the foreman's daughter from the estate up in the mountains. At sixteen the two of them had paraded arm-in-arm during Carnaval while onlookers drenched them with buckets of water. Had he married her, Ignacio might have become a foreman himself, supervising other men's labour rather than trying to sell them bars of soap, rolls of toilet paper, straw hats and dry biscuits. But he had returned to the village on the canyon floor to build the two-room house onto the back of his father's shop, and Juana had cast her spell on him. When she sauntered past the shop, her basket swaying on her head (who knew what powders and potions she had sprinkled over the twisted wicker), Ignacio would straighten up from his masonry. His father, folded onto the overturned box he used as a stool from which to direct his son's toil, would beat his cane against the brown dust. He ordered Ignacio back to work. The longing stares his son directed at young women normally wrung cackles from the old man's throat, but this time, her grandmother said, he seemed to detect the danger of Juana's dipping strides. Day after day she sidled past the emerging rough walls of the house. Juana washed clothes in the river and returned them to her mother's hut. She wandered by carrying the baskets of fruit she sold to passengers on the microbus that hurtled down the highway on its way to Quito. The microbus stopped on the edge of the village three times a day, giving Juana six more opportunities to torment Ignacio with her long-limbed gait. He did not see her out at the highway, her grandmother said, shoving her rotting fruit into passengers' faces as she clawed back the other *negritas* and whined: —*Cómpreme, cómpreme.*— All Ignacio knew of Juana was the arrogant length of her body shimmering out of the dusty canyon heat four, six or eight times a day.

—It's the foreman's daughter who should have been your mother, her grandmother said. —Then you would have been a nice-looking girl, not a dark, ugly thing.—

In the canyon nights the damp chill of the house's stone and mortar numbs her fingers. Marta and her grandmother sleep on cots in the outer room. Her grandmother hardly sleeps. Long into the night she squats on her rickety haunches on the edge of her cot, clucking incantations in Quichua as she tries to break the spell Juana has cast on her son. Marta dozes until the paired rhythmic breaths begin to flow from the inner room. She wakes, drives her palms against her ears. A few moments later her mother's yowls lash the icy stone. Her grandmother cuts short her exorcisms. —*Tutahucha,* she spits. Marta recognizes the Quichua compound: night-sin. —Every night. It's not normal. The demons are inside her.—

She crosses herself, offers the darkness a prayer in Spanish, then resumes muttering in Quichua. When Marta wakes in the morning her grandmother is sleeping in a hunched posture, her cord-like lips agape. Marta hurries out of bed to feel her grandmother's shins, exposed beneath the drawn-up hems of her layered skirts. Her grandfather died during the night. For old people, she thinks, night means death; adults such as her parents, on the other hand, become invested with supernatural life. Every night she wrestles with shame and confusion.

As she watches them during the day, she wonders whether anybody else knows. Ignacio manages the shop with callused, capable hands that weigh bags of rice and potatoes and count out wrinkled *sucre* notes. His hair is receding. He is the only man in the village who wears glasses. Would the hard little women who snarl at her mother's blackness continue to respect him if they knew what happened in the house at night? Or do they snarl because they know? If her mother is possessed, her father must share Juana's evil. Her grandmother says the spell that Juana has cast on him makes Ignacio an accomplice to her mother's devilry. Marta shudders at the thought of the destiny that awaits them. Each night she waits for the rising tide of interlocked breathing; only after it has peaked in her mother's moans can she pray herself to sleep. How can her parents be so foolhardy? Haven't they heard Father Alberto in the windswept church on Sunday morning declaiming that he who fails to cast out the devil from his soul will burn in Hell forever? Look at the sun, commands Father Alberto, his voice rasping from twenty years of exhorting the village to spiritual rectitude. Within the core of the sun flames a second sun, boiling red with all the devil's juices. Imagine that this sun plunged to earth, bore down on your flesh and scorched you through everlasting damnation. That is what Hell is like. Only Hell is worse than that, because the sun at the earth's core is a million times hotter and more potent than the sun in the heavens.

And it is not merely your flesh that will be seared, but the fibre of your soul. And it will never end.

That is what her parents are risking.

Yet despite her grandmother's wistful memories of the foreman's daughter, she would not wish to be another couple's child. No doubt if Ignacio had married another woman she would be prettier, lighter skinned, wear newer shoes. But what if Juana had married another man? Or failed to marry him? Her grandmother never mentions this possibility. Juana is not certain of her father's identity: none of the three or four leading candidates was eager to claim paternity. When Marta prays she gives thanks for having been granted two living, acknowledged parents. Her father is the most respected man in the village, her mother the prettiest woman. None of the children who ridicule her mixed parentage can say the same.

She is Juana and Ignacio's only living child. Her grandmother mumbles that had Juana prayed more diligently Marta's brother and sisters might have lived. Juana saunters through her daily chores oblivious to her mother-in-law's accusations. With an easy nonchalance she heats potatoes, shakes out dusty clothes, tells Marta to go to the river to collect buckets of water to soak down the dust in front of the door. Juana's limbs slide through the bright sunlight with a silky grace that strikes Marta as being at odds with demonic possession: the devil, she has gleaned from Father Alberto's sermons, makes you frenzied. Yet thinking of the rushed panting that will break from her parents' bedroom after dark, she feels her nervousness returning. At every chance she scurries away from her chores and follows the edge of the highway up the slope to the church.

The church stands on a knoll above the village, shrivelled by the lifeless canyon walls. Beyond the top of the canyon, Ignacio has told her, lies the bleak green of the *páramo*, where on a clear day snow-draped volcanoes shine in the bright air. The windblown sand covers the village like a shifting cape; the houses poke through in wedged protrusions. But on the hillside dominated by the church and the cemetery the earth is so bare and hard packed that it takes a team of men from the village half a day to dig a grave. Children's graves are smaller, and Marta is certain that the graves of Juan, Ana and Isabel could not have taken long to dig. Two of the wooden crosses have toppled over and a third stands askew. It doesn't matter; their faces shine before her eyes: Juan chubby cheeked and wearing glasses like her father; Ana pretty with long hair and a passion for games; Isabel pudgy, shy, dark skinned. Being younger than her, they listen to her with respect. She crouches on her knees in the grit. The dry canyon wind snaps at the dress she has been wearing since last Sunday.

—It's very windy today and Mami sent me to the river three times for water to keep down the dust. When the dust blows into the house it gets into the beds and onto the plates and knives. The potatoes taste of dust. The dust makes Grandmother's cough worse. Papi says we must respect Grandmother even though she says nasty things. She is old and she is going to die soon, and then you will meet her in Heaven. You'll see how difficult she can be. Do you want to play? Let's all play together.—

She springs to her feet and dances around the barren cemetery, weaving between the lurching wooden crosses perched on the low mounds. Singing under her breath, she skips as far as the tall family tomb left behind, only half of its slots filled, by the wealthy clan that used to own everything in the village. She halts to catch her breath and Ana, her brown eyes shining in the sunlight, almost grabs her arm. With a shriek, Marta yells: —You can't catch me!—

She pelts flat-out across the cemetery.

—Little girl! shouts Father Alberto.

She falls to her knees. Crouching on all fours, she stares across her brother and sisters' graves at his eroded form stretching up against the blue sky. The wind rushing through his sparse grey hair burns her face.

—This is a sacred place. Go to the river, where the other children play.—

She scrambles to her feet. A stinging runs from her knee up to her right shoulder; an eddy of red seeps through the grey grit caking her knee where she fell. She begins to sob. Her tears, drying almost before they can begin to flow, give her face a stretched feel. She ducks her head away from the wind. —I was playing with my brother and my sisters. They can't come to the river.—

—Your brother and sisters are with Our Father in Heaven, my daughter. They were fortunate to die while they were innocent. You must pray that you will be worthy of joining them when your life on this earth is done.—

—Yes, Father.— Her knee aches. She hears the sound of a distant engine: the second microbus of the day rushes across the valley floor. Her mother will be out at the highway, fighting back the other women to thrust her basket of fruit into the passengers' faces. —Father Alberto, will you take my confession?—

The priest's sharp jaw stiffens. The wind flails his cassock about. —I'm not in the confessional now, little girl.

Do you think I should do for you what I don't do for others? Are you succumbing to the sin of self-love?—

He hurries her out of the cemetery, growling at her to let her dead rest in peace. —Goodbye, Juan. Goodbye, Ana. Goodbye, Isabel. *Hasta la próxima.*—

She limps home. Her mother returns from the highway and sends her down to the river to collect a bucket of water to clean her knee.

Two ⚏

All week she prepares her confession. It is important to speak clearly to Father Alberto. He can mould reality: a slip of his hand changed her name. The María to which Ignacio and Juana had agreed at her grandmother's insistence (a godless marriage must make one concession to sanctity) became Marta when Father Alberto let the tip of the *i* slide up too high and crossed it. Once the name had been entered in the church registry, it was too late. Father Alberto baptized her as Marta and her parents, fearing his scorn and the vengeance of the God who stood behind him, conformed. —Why he couldn't have corrected it, why he couldn't have allowed you to take the Holy Mother's name, I don't understand, her grandmother says, shaking her scrawny head. —That priest is the nastiest man in the village.—

By denying her the Virgin's name, he has selected her for some other destiny: she has been marked out for an extraordinary life. On Saturday evening, silently rehearsing her confession, she asks her grandmother: —Why was I chosen to survive? Why not one of the others?—

—You're the firstborn, her grandmother says. —You were a novelty. With the others your devil of a mother got bored. She wandered off while they were crying to be fed,

she left them outside where the sun burned them and the
flies crawled over them. The demons are inside her!—

Marta rolls over in her cot. She stares into the blackness,
waiting for the sound of her parents' cries.

In the morning, when her turn to kneel on the worn
wood of the confessional arrives, she holds her breath
inside her chest for a long moment before expelling it in
a rush: —Forgive me, Father, for I have sinned.—

—Yes, my daughter?—

She feels the toes of her decaying canvas sneakers bending behind her. —I hear demons. Every night. I wait for
them.—

—Demons?—

—Please don't tell anyone, Father. Mami and Papi have
demons inside them — my grandmother says it's Mami's
fault, that she's possessed. Please don't tell anyone. Grandmother and I wait for the demons every night.—

—Every night?—

—Yes, Father. *Todas las noches.*—

The priest sighs. —Anything else, my daughter?—

—Does that mean I'll be possessed too, Father?—

—Yes, if you grow up to be like your mother!— His voice
trembles. —You must strive to be as innocent as your
brothers and sisters. You must fix their angelic goodness
in your mind . . . Anything else, little girl?—

—The . . . the sin of self-love, she recites, stumbling over
the words.

—How did you commit this sin?—

Astonished and disappointed, she thinks: doesn't he
remember? —I was chosen to survive, to do something
special.—

—You are mistaken, little girl. It is your brother and
sisters who have been chosen by Our Lord to join him in

Heaven. They are special. You He has abandoned to the shame and suffering of life on this earth. Humble yourself. Make yourself meek and good. Guard your purity more ferociously than you guard your life. *Bienaventurados sean los mansos, que de ellos será el reino de los cielos.*—

He assigns her twice as many Hail Mary's as he has ever imposed on her before, and dismisses her from the confessional. Ignacio and Juana have returned to the house, but her grandmother waits for her outside the splintered church door. —You had a lot to confess today, Marta.—

—*Harto, abuelita.* I was trying to get rid of the demons.—

That night, unable to sleep, she sits up in her cot and listens to her grandmother's Quichua incantations. She tries to repeat the grumbled phrases. Riddled with deep-throated pops and larded with soft explosions of air, the chain of syllables tires her. She drops off to sleep with her grandmother's language in her mouth.

She wakes in the morning filled with a sprightly happiness, rolls out of bed, strokes her grandmother's exposed shins and stops short: the shins are cold. Her grandmother lies curled and stiffened on her narrow cot. No sound comes from her parents' room. When she walks to the door white fog, spilling down from the *páramo*, has wiped away the streets. She listens to the river flowing through the silence.

THREE ♪

N ext day at her grandmother's funeral the weather
remains grey and windless. Father Alberto presides
with embittered piety. He describes Marta's grandmother as a strong woman in a tone that reminds everyone
present of his hatred of her. Marta glances towards her
father. Ignacio, whom grief seems to have rendered pudg-
ier, balder, more blinkered behind his glasses, stares at his
dented, over-polished shoes. Juana is whistling a soft tune
under her breath.

The rough-hewn cross which Ignacio has fashioned for
his mother by dismantling a shelf in the back of the shop
is planted next to the cross marking the resting place of
Marta's grandfather. The twin grave lies only a few steps
from where Juan, Ana and Isabel are buried. In the days
after the funeral, Marta discovers that she can no longer
speak to her sisters and brother. The forbidding presence
of her grandmother strikes them silent. Early one morning, when she hopes that Father Alberto will be in bed,
she dances a slow spiral around the graves. They refuse to
spring up from the earth to play with her. The hiss of
Quichua whispers drives her out of the cemetery. She
retreats to the house. Ignacio has folded up her grandmother's cot, carried it around the building to the shop

and attached a price tag to one leg. At night the outer
room of the house is hers alone. She moves her cot into
the corner farthest from the inner room, makes a barricade
of two cardboard boxes and settles down into a space that
feels too large for her. She has always seen her parents
obscured, as if through muddied water, by her grandmother's judgements and explanations. After the funeral
she faces them for the first time. Ignacio and Juana become
nagging and unpredictable, alternately too remote to be
human and suffocatingly close and dictatorial.

Marta's body is changing shape: she feels wrenched out
of herself. Her breasts swell without attaining the fullness
of her mother's; her neck sprouts, yet remains stubby by
comparison with Juana's. She realizes that she has inherited something of Ignacio's low-slung bulk; she will never
attain Juana's leggy grace or match her slinky, slumberous
gait. But what does it matter? She has started to bleed. She
could get married and have a baby, put Ignacio and Juana
behind her. She must have been crazy ever to have thought
of her mother as beautiful. When she watches Juana now,
Marta notices her ugly teeth, the drooping flesh at either
side of her thick-lipped mouth, the dullness of her eyes.
Above all, she sees her mother's blackness. The village
women's words about the stupidity of *negritas* ring through
her mind. Feeling contaminated, she lashes out at Juana.
Why are you so lazy? Why are you so scatterbrained and
simple-minded and annoying? Juana, preferring the company of the women who sell fruit to microbus passengers,
forgets to return for her shift in the shop. Marta remains
stranded at the counter for hours.

Some mornings she awakes to find that Juana has already
sauntered down to the highway. Ignacio is out making a
deal to buy potatoes or sell seeds, and the shop stands

unattended. Marta runs down the street to the school, pokes her head in the door to explain to the *maestra* that she cannot come today because she must work in the shop and rushes back over the gritty sand, tears churning up in her eyes at her mother's negligence. One day she can no longer be bothered to run down the street to excuse herself; she loses the habit of going to school. Only one other girl of her age still comes to class. When girls cease to be children, the schoolmistress says, there remains little to teach them.

Loose sand blows down the street outside the shop; customers are scarce. Alone together among the splintered, half-stocked shelves, she and Ignacio bicker. He grunts at her to dust the merchandise, to rearrange bags or boxes on the shelves; he uses a tone better suited to addressing a dog than a daughter. His tubby body and deep stoop, the oddly spherical skull revealed by the hairline sliding ever higher up his forehead, his thick glasses and the limp, filthy tie he persists in wearing over his rumpled shirts, cry out for mockery. She hates his thick fingers, his gruff jealousy of the lingering stares men who enter the shop turn upon her. When she rebuffs his order to sweep the floor for the third time that day, he repeats himself in an arrogant, mechanical drone. His head remains bowed.

—Do it yourself, she says.

—*¡Carajo*, you're a stupid girl! Is that all you ever learned at school? To insult your father?—

—Stupid fathers deserve to be insulted.— She feels awed by her own bravado. Fright startles her as she detects the slow stirring behind his glasses.

Ignacio swears, seizing the broom from her hands. He breaks the shaft in two over the counter. His glasses slip down to the end of his nose. Flailing the jagged shard of the broomstick, he lunges at her. At close range he becomes towering and heavy chested. His brawny mass slams her back against a shelf loaded with bags of stale biscuits. His fingers clamp shut around her wrist. Terror flashes through her: she struggles. He wrenches her arm behind her back and rams her face into the dry creases of the biscuit bags. The thudding crack of the broomstick across her buttocks makes her shriek. His second blow, catching her across the backs of her legs, crumples her to the ground. Sand grinds into her cheeks; Ignacio wrenches her arm up and around until she is certain that it will snap from its socket. She screams through her tears as the broomstick strikes her hip, pounding against almost unprotected bone. Her wails gust against the walls like the cries on fiesta nights, when drunken men beat their wives. Ignacio has recognized her womanhood: each bruising thud contains an acknowledgement. The mounting pressure in her bladder breaks: a jet of hot liquid dashes down her legs and turns cold.

—Disgusting little whore! Ignacio shouts, his blows subsiding as he waves the broomstick shard at the dark patch on the sand.

She huddles against the base of the shelves. Sobs pull through her exhausted body, shaking her as though trying to toss off the soreness in her legs and hips and buttocks. The pain flees deep inside her, gnawing at her bones. She writhes in a vain effort to elude it. The metallic smack of cold urine smearing her legs mingles with the smell of dried-out planks. When night falls, they come and lift her off the cold sand. Fingers squeeze her armpits, hands grip her ankles. She slumps into her cot, her blankets are pulled over her. Ana's brown eyes peer at her through the darkness. They are playing a breathless game of tag in the cemetery. Her grandmother watches them with a smile, speaking words they cannot understand.

The howling chill of the night wrings her awake. Rising moans, the familiar bounding shriek. —Oh, Ignacio, how it burns! . . .—

Marta sinks deeper into the flesh muffling her bones, a withdrawal more profound than sleep. Her parents no longer make love every night, so why this night? How can they dash aside her suffering? When darkness overcomes her it has a twisty, buffeting force alien to sleep. She dances around and around with Ana and Isabel and Juan. Isabel is growing up, her baby fat dropping away; soon they will be three pretty sisters. Juan, restrained but strong, will kill any man who tries to harm them. He will kill Ignacio if he must. Together the four of them forge a path to Heaven. That is where the rich people live. They promenade through the cool, snowy streets of Heaven and the crowds flock to greet them, assuring them that here, no matter how sick or wounded a girl may be, no one will hurt her.

Daylight disturbs her ears as well as her eyes. The hiss and crackle of the fire, the clank of Juana's iron pots and tin spoons, the distant roar of the microbus out on the highway, the rasp of wind-driven sand and the splat of buckets of water being emptied to hold the sand at bay: she rolls her head against the pillow.

Father Alberto, his throat puckered and lank, stands over her cot. —It is time for you to confess your sins, my daughter.—

—Am I going to die, Father?—

—You have not come to church for two weeks. You are burdened with sin. You must confess.—

His knobbly shoulders rise and fall. Each breath he draws is followed by a straining hiss, a sort of after-breath. Not having noticed this before, she stares at him until his hard scrutiny brings her back to herself. —I have nothing to confess.—

—You have disobeyed your father. God will scorch your soul in hellfire unless you unburden yourself and beg his forgiveness.—

The dry gush of his after-breath frays the silence. Avoiding his furious stare, she focuses on a point above and beyond his lean, eroded features. In the shadows of the scrap-tin patchwork of the ceiling nestle the fading faces of her sisters and brother, the blank gaze of Juana's indifference, the resentful glare Ignacio directed towards her yesterday morning. The priest paces the dirt floor. He pulls up an overturned crate and seats himself next to her cot. His hands fumble with impatience. —I don't know why I accepted this posting. They said: 'Go there for five years, it'll be good experience.' They said they'd send me to the coast after that. I could go boating through the lianas, I could walk on the beach and eat fresh fish. And then they left me here for twenty years. If I'd known they were going to abandon me, I would have given up my vocation.—

Feeling bidden to speak but unable to meet his eyes, she murmurs: —I must get away from here. I'm the only one who survived, Father. I must live enough for four.—

—You must be pure enough for four. You must stifle the sin of self-love.—

—You changed my name. If my name can be changed, so can the rest of me.—

—That is blasphemy! You are as God created you.— He stands up. —Look at me, little girl. Look into my eyes!—

She twists her head around on the pillow, staring at the far wall of the room. When he leans over her in a whiff of foul-smelling breath and rank cassock, she squeezes her eyes shut. His voice rises in a grumbled, incantatory mutter. He is praying over her. His words are incomprehensible; he has reverted to the priest's language in which her grandmother told her they were taught to pray in the old days. Her eyes half closed, she endures the stuttering rain of syllables. She hears him finish and pick his way towards the door.

—The devil has entered her body, he says to Ignacio and Juana. —I glimpsed Satan in the corner of her eye, but he turned her head before I could drive him out. You have a long struggle before you. This girl's soul has been imperilled for many years. She once confessed to me that she and her grandmother waited for demons at night.—

The devil? Marta trembles beneath her blankets. Has she been crying out at night like Juana? But that takes a man and she has never . . . The thought of being with a man flushes her cheeks with heat and turns her stomach queasy. —It's not true! she shouts, sitting up in bed. — There's no devil in me. Revolting old man! ¡*Asqueroso!*—

With a clench of his shoulders, the priest spits. A large translucent gob smacks against the strut of her cot. — You've inherited all your grandmother's devilry!—

He stumps out into the street.

Juana bursts out laughing. She hurries over to the cot, enfolding Marta in her warm arms. But before Marta can hug her back, Juana has sprung away to regale Ignacio with filthy stories about Father Alberto.

—You know how he keeps his vows of chastity? she asks. —They saw him up on the *páramo* rutting with an alpaca! —

Ignacio responds with a sad smile. Marta, leaning forward in her cot, tries to catch his attention. He turns away and walks into the street without meeting her eyes.

FOUR

ours skim over her as she lies in the cot. One day
she hobbles across the dirt floor to bake the potatoes while Juana slouches down to the river to fill
buckets with water. Juana no longer goes out to meet the
microbus each time it roars down the highway; her basket
sits abandoned on the off-balance kitchen table. Tossing
on her cot, Marta listens for the whine of the microbus's
engine. Something has changed. The microbus still passes
the village three times a day, but the sound of its engine
rises as it approaches, begins to fade, then falls out of
earshot. The day has been knocked out of shape.

Over supper Ignacio, his mouth full of potatoes, tells
Juana that the army construction crew has arrived. From
now on the microbus will stop one kilometre beyond the
village, at the spot where the military control post is to be
built. The soldiers will spend a month camped outside the
village. Their presence will mean good business for the
shop. Ignacio has spoken to the lieutenant in charge of the
crew; he has agreed to bring the men around to the shop
on payday, provided that he can buy at a discount. —We're
going to need more staff, Ignacio mumbles, not looking at
Marta. —For the nights when the soldiers come.—

Marta gazes at the dirt floor. If this is the closest he can come to an apology, she will never again set foot in the shop.

To compensate for shirking her duties in the shop, she works all day in the house. She cleans and cooks until her back aches and her cheeks feel leathery from bending close to the fire. Ignacio has not addressed a word to her in weeks, yet he is confronted with her worth every evening when he stumbles in from the shop to a swept floor and scorching hot potatoes. How he will regret having mistreated her! If only she could hear what he says to Father Alberto in the confessional!

Father Alberto's commands to submit to God's will, to preserve the form in which God created her, make Marta shake with anger. The need to become someone else harries her from her sleep. She is not María but Marta; not dead like her sisters and brother, but alive and changing.

The bending and stretching of her housework strengthens her battered leg. As her hobble dwindles to a barely noticeable limp, Juana sends her to the river again to collect water. Down at the river all talk is of the soldiers. They have set up their camp on the dry spur known as El Lomito. They work all day under the orders of the lieutenant. Their tunics unbuttoned, they dig foundations, mix cement in battered wheelbarrows, shift loads of dirt from one side of the highway to the other. Many girls have invented errands to justify a visit to the soldiers' camp. Laughing debates play across the rushing brown water as the girls discuss whether it is better to visit in the midday heat when the men open their shirts (—Shameless! the *maestra*'s daughter howls as her neighbour describes the advantages of a midday visit), or in the evening when their uniforms have been fastened and straightened to parade-ground correctness.

—They look great in their uniforms, says a girl who is beating a sodden, lathered dress against a rock. —Nobody in this shitty village ever wears a uniform.—

—They're all so short, complains a tall black woman named Hortensia. Two or three other black women nod in agreement. Marta imagines what her mother, never at a loss for a lewd comment, would have to say about the liabilities of the soldiers' shortness. She learns that, except for the tall overweight lieutenant, most of the soldiers are peasants from up on the *páramo*. Indians in uniform, one woman moans; who gives a damn about Indians?

—They'd be just right for this little one, Hortensia says, her glance alighting on Marta. —You're lucky you're not as tall as your mami. You'll fit those peasants perfectly!— She laughs with a thrust of her hips. A volley of giggles flutters over the smoke-brown surface of the water as Marta fills her bucket and trails home.

She does not fake an errand to visit the soldiers' camp. She sticks to the house, completing her chores at the river as quickly as she can. On Friday evenings, and all day on Saturdays, she hears the soldiers' voices booming through the wall from the back of the shop. Ignacio, working late, comes home frustrated and disgruntled. He is selling more merchandise than ever before, but the soldiers have destroyed his self-esteem. The most respected man in the village, he has been pummelled with abuse, crude jokes, sarcastic remarks ridiculing his puny, ill-stocked little shop. Eighteen-year-old peasant boys whose Quichua accents slur their Spanish r's into trilled z's have lectured him on the wonderful bars and boutiques of Quito and Guayaquil.

The lieutenant, whom he took to be his friend, has tolerated and even contributed to these outrages.

Juana shrugs her shoulders as Ignacio pours out his unhappiness. The microbus stops so far from the village now, she says. She can hardly be bothered to walk all that way. At least the soldiers are good customers: they would gobble oranges and bananas all day if the lieutenant allowed it. Yes, they're good boys, the soldiers; it's too bad they'll be going back to Quito in a couple of weeks.

—Yes, I bet you like them, Ignacio says, the sudden weight of his forearms jolting the flimsy table. —I bet they whistle at your ass.—

—So they whistle. So what? I can't stop them whistling, can I?—

Juana stands up. Her mouth twists. Marta feels that she is seeing the texture of her mother's skin for the first time. Juana's dingy dress, the slack darkness beneath her eyes, the flea-bitten legs moving with slovenly grace as she turns away from the table: the physical fact of her mother's life clubs her senses. She imagines how it must feel to be married to Ignacio, baffled by the world, blithely indifferent to her husband's seriousness yet troubled by the gap between their outlooks. As she collects the dirty dishes, Marta grows acutely conscious of the way her own arms flow from her shoulders, her legs from her hips. She looks down at her feet, holding her hands against her sides.

Her father is growling into the tabletop, spoiling for a fight. But she no longer feels driven to torment him. She gets up from the table.

She sings while she washes the dishes. If she passed Father Alberto in the street (him or one of the pious women who cross themselves and grunt insults at her when they meet), she could explain with absolute confidence why she does not attend Mass. She has not stopped believing in God: He breathes from every rock and lizard-filled cranny in the village. It is not out of fear of Ignacio or hatred of Father Alberto; it is not because of sin or devil worship. She has refused to return to Mass because she has become aware that she is a different sort of person from the other people in this village. She is special: the daughter of the most important man and the prettiest woman. *Bienaventurados sean los mansos* . . . She is not meek. She cannot live her life squashed by self-denial: the three crosses in the cemetery urge her to seize every instant of existence with clenched fists. She must become on the outside the kind of woman she feels blossoming inside her.

FIVE ℊ

The construction crew falls behind on its work. The boisterous weekends in the shop continue for another month. Then the work is finished and one morning at dawn the soldiers climb into the back of a large military truck and rumble away to Quito. The vitality of the women's riverbank conversation ebbs. But there is a new source of interest: a sergeant and three soldiers have arrived to maintain the post. The four men live in a small barracks behind the administrative office on the western edge of the highway. During the day they regulate the traffic, collect passenger lists from the three daytime microbuses, search for contraband in the trucks that roll down the highway. On Saturday evenings those who are off duty wander into the village in search of company. The sergeant is a thin, desolate-looking man in his forties who rarely speaks; but the three soldiers, nervous boys in their late teens, are far from home and eager to talk.

Marta's leg has recovered. Her limp returns only when she is tired. Feeling hemmed in by the dark outer room of the house, she escapes to the river to talk to the other women and girls. Minutes spin into hours as she squats chatting on a sandy bluff. Even the older women listen to her opinions now, giving her their full attention. She arrives home late and scrambles to get the potatoes ready before Ignacio and Juana return.

Juana comes home despondent. The new control post is too far from the village; she is selling less and less fruit. She is fed up with pitting her stamina against that of young girls. —Before the microbus pulled in and pulled out. It was the quickest girl who got the sale. Now the stops take hours. The soldiers check documents, the passengers stretch their legs, the *señoras* go in and use the toilet. You have to keep following them around. It's too much bother for me, girl.—

She stands up and tilts back her head, parted lips baring her uneven teeth. All the secret sags in her face have swarmed to the surface. Marta notices how the slackness has shaken down into Juana's neck, depriving her throat of its old elegant curve. Juana holds out the basket. —You can't spend your whole life in the house, girl. I'm sick of selling fruit. Tomorrow you go.—

In the icy dawn Ignacio presents her with fresh oranges and guavas. He always gets the best fruit. Where the other women rely on the unkempt grotto half an hour's walk upriver from the village, Ignacio has his fruit driven up in a truck once a week from the sugar cane valley far below. He loads the wicker basket for her. In the cold morning light, his hands look pudgy and benign.

—Keep following them around, Juana says, chewing on her hard breakfast roll. —Show them that nice fruit.—

—If she doesn't sell it, Ignacio announces, addressing no one in particular, I won't have money to buy more fruit next week.—

She stumbles out the door. The sun has risen, but the air remains frigid. She wanders in the direction of the rise at the end of the village. Her basket of fruit, clutched against her stomach, weighs down on her forearms. The imbalance makes her feel ungainly. It strains her back. She meanders to a halt.

—¡*La cabeza!* her mother's voice shrieks down the street. —Carry it on your head!—

She hesitates, hoists the basket onto her crown, takes a few tentative steps and finds she can hold the fruit steady against her forward momentum with one upstretched open hand. She feels like a reveller on a festival day demonstrating a dance step. Her uphooked arm and straightened spine confer upon her body a complicated geometry of which she is at first self-conscious and then proud. She skims down the street, longing to be seen. She imagines Juana standing outside the door of the house admiring her graceful departure. The thought calls up childhood memories of crouching in the doorway while Juana trailed down to the river to do the laundry. But when she risks a backward glance, Juana has disappeared.

Six ✠

S he gets to the top of the gritty brown slope just in time to see the microbus roar away. She stares at the control post and the three tall black women who are retreating from the highway. The buildings' shiny newness drains her of her self-confidence. The control post has been built at the peak of El Lomito; beyond it the highway drops into a gully before beginning the long ascent of the southern wall of the canyon. To her left, on the eastern verge of the highway, stands a concrete pillbox. A young soldier slumps on a stool inside. She has just started forward again when she notices his scrutiny. He is observing her in a way village boys have taught her to recognize: the aggressive, deprecating, ingratiating stare of a man who is appraising a woman's body. She teeters to a halt. Her stomach breaks into small pieces, which rearrange themselves in an indigestible shape. When she draws her next breath the taper of her body feels equal to the young soldier's hunger, although the arm she has looped up over her head to steady her basket of fruit has begun to seem like a contrivance. Is she tempting him? She hates him for his predatory gaze; she longs for him to like her. She walks quickly, looking straight ahead. She is approaching the horizontal bar, stretched across the highway, that stops the traffic for inspection. On the western, right-hand verge stands the main complex of the control post: a large whitewashed building whose flat roof protrudes into an overhang supported by two uprights. The three black women, Hortensia standing in the middle, watch her from the bench in the shadow of the overhang. Behind them she glimpses swinging doors, a glassed-in entrance hall, smaller doors with polished doorhandles implanted in the inside walls of the building. The glossy shine of the place, with all its strange angles and hinges and gleams, stuns her.

—Juana's sent her daughter, Hortensia's voice rings from the shadow. —Little Marta's come to see the soldier boys.—

Bowing her head, she seats herself on the bench. — Mami doesn't want to come any more. She says she's too old for this.—

Her words quell the women's mockery. Juana too old? But she's their age! They eye Marta with wary looks.

—She's come to drive us into our graves, Hortensia says. —Here, little daughter, let me see what you're selling.—

She plucks Marta's overflowing basket from her grasp, appraising the piles of fresh oranges and guavas. —¡Mierda! Pure shit! Look at this. Anybody who eats it will die of fever.— She flings an orange into the dirt. —And these guavas – inedible! – She hurls two guavas in quick succession into the pebbly grit.

—No! Marta cries, as the guavas' skins open in white gashes against the brown dust. Hortensia grabs a third guava. Marta springs towards her, trying to wrest the basket from her grasp. Hortensia holds on. With a gleeful hoot, she upends the basket, spilling Marta's fruit onto the ground. The other two women double over with laughter.

Marta rushes forward and rakes her fingernails down Hortensia's giggling cheeks. Diving across the taller woman's lap, she sweeps Hortensia's bag of miserable, wrinkled fruit onto the ground. She dances with rage, kicking and stamping Hortensia's apples and guavas with her sneakers. Hortensia flings herself at Marta. They thud to the ground and scrabble in the dirt. She shrieks as Hortensia's teeth clamp into her cheek. The intrusive, mauling bite paralyzes Marta; her slaps at Hortensia's face and shoulders grow feeble. She hears doors bursting open, thumping boots. Square brown hands fitted to long khaki arms haul Hortensia to her feet. A man digs his fist into Hortensia's stomach, doubling her over. The second soldier knees her in the ass, ramming her into the wall. She collapses onto the bench and wheezes for breath. The other two women flee around the corner of the building. Terror banishing her sobs, Marta tries to stagger after them. She has just managed to struggle to her feet when the second soldier's hand sweeps around. He steps in front of her, driving his fist forward. Dirt wheels up from behind and cracks against the back of her head. Fiery lines radiate from the centre of her skull, lashing through her jaw. Probing with her tongue, she finds a tooth dangling by a thread. She pries it free, spits it out. The tip of her tongue caresses a ragged rawness: the touch sets her skull singing. She gropes into a sitting position and forages in the dust for her tooth. She shuts her palm tight and holds on against the ringing waves, letting her tears rise into a lament that is part incantation. —*Pachamama,* she murmurs in her grandmother's voice. —*Pachamama, Pachamama . . .* —

—*¡Putas de mierda!* shouts the soldier who flung Hortensia into the wall. —It's the Army that gives the orders at this control post. If you want to sell your shit here, then

you'll do so as the Army commands! You're lucky the
sergeant's in his quarters. If he had heard this . . . —

—She's the troublemaker, Hortensia breaks in, jab-
bing her finger at Marta. —She's possessed by the devil,
she doesn't go to Mass, she won't confess her sins. The
priest . . . —

—Screw the priest, says the soldier who knocked out
Marta's tooth. Staring past his partner, he fixes Hortensia
with an angry glare. —We don't give a fuck about your
priests. We're Evangelical Christians. We piss on priests
and confessions and superstitions.—

—You're not Catholic? Marta says. —You belong to
another religion?—

—That's right.— The soldier smirks. For a moment she
fears he will punch her again. He orders Marta and Hortensia to clean up the spilled fruit and go home for the day.
—You can come back tomorrow, provided you conduct
yourselves in an orderly fashion.—

—I'm never going back, Marta moans to Juana, once
she has sobbed out her story.

—Come on girl, we need the money.—

—Then you go.—

Juana bends over the cooking fire. After a few moments
she starts whistling a tune.

The throbbing in Marta's face keeps her awake long
after Juana and Ignacio have gone to bed. If she returns
to the control post, Hortensia will kill her. And she has
lost a tooth. She is ugly, ugly! No man will want to marry
her. In the darkness she practises drawing back her lips,
trying to judge how widely she can smile without revealing
the blemish. Her bruised, stiffening cheek aches. The
soldier in the pillbox wouldn't spare her a glance now. A
tremor shivers through her as she thinks of the two men

bold enough to call themselves *evangélicos.* To scorn
Father Alberto! To say so with pride! A current of energy
rushes through her: she feels herself on the brink of a
marvellous discovery. The thought of men who call themselves Christians yet disdain priests baffles and tantalizes
her. She falls asleep in the icy depths of the night wondering whether the soldier in the pillbox is a Catholic or an
Evangelical.

In the morning, pleading illness, she refuses to leave
her cot. Her parents grumble and look away. Through
her stiff, swollen face, she asks: —Papi, do these soldiers
go to church?—

He looks up from behind his thick glasses. —Only the
sergeant. The sergeant's a decent man. The young ones
are like you. They're too arrogant to listen to Father
Alberto. They sing hymns together in their barracks. Singing! You'd think they were women!—

The next morning Marta is awake before sunrise. She
dresses, prepares her basket of fruit and eats her morning
roll on the way to the control post. This morning the
soldier who hit her sits in the pillbox; the one who stared
at her spends the day inside. Five other women tramp up
the hillside carrying their wares; one of them is selling
cans of Coca-Cola.

They sit down to await the first microbus of the day.
There is no sign of Hortensia.

The first day she sells nothing. The older women out-
flank Marta at every turn. They pursue the passengers with
lowing groans. —*Cómpreme, cómpreme, señor.*— They block
the paths of the passengers who climb down from the
microbus, dogging the heels of the women who enter the
glassed-in corridor of the main building to use the toilet.
She feels shy and clumsy. What will the soldier who stared

at her think if she abases herself like these other women?
She is proud; she is the girl who has defied Father Alberto.
But the first clutch of *sucres* passed to her in exchange for
a brace of oranges calms her. The pleasure of folding the
notes in her palm, slipping them into her pocket rather
than into the top drawer of Ignacio's shop counter, fills
her with self-assurance. When she presents her earnings
to Juana and Ignacio in the evening, she feels herself
growing larger. The strength that comes from knowing
that they rely on her earnings sends her plunging forward
into the next day. She elbows aside the other women,
shoves her fruit in the passengers' faces, insisting on the
superior freshness of her guavas and bananas and oranges.
She does not beg. She holds her voice under control,
refusing to make herself pathetic. It is not desperation that
motivates her, but energy. She bubbles through the long
days, cajoling tired passengers into buying her wares, teasing the other women, gossiping with the soldiers.

In less than a month she has become the centre of life
at the control post. Aware of the rifts her fight with Hortensia has opened up (Hortensia has not returned to the
control post), she is careful to avoid arousing the other
women's hostility. She smiles at everyone. Even after a
microbus loaded with bluejeaned gringos has sent them
crawling over each other in the battle for easy money,
Marta keeps her conversation light and jokey. She seizes
upon budding quarrels like splinters, plucking them out
with a joke before they can fester. The other women have
begun to fuss over her; like a horde of proud mothers,
they boast of her sales ability. —Look at little Marta, they
call to the soldiers. —She grew up in a shop; she's spent
her whole life selling.—

She is astonished by the person she is becoming. She pursues fresh wonders every day, eager to discover where they will lead her.

¶

The girl in the village dreamed of a world glistening like glass. The woman in the city, spraying the curve of her bay window with a plastic bottle fitted with a squeeze-cap, then scrubbing the pane until she is dazzled by the glare of a short lawn of snow, grows bored with commonplace luxuries.

Where did I come from? As she grows older the question forces itself on her. It is a child's question, a question María might have asked her as an infant; so why does the shadow of middle age summon it back? What compels her to relive the journey of the young foreigner who brought her here? It would be more comfortable to bury the past, to return to her housework, to look for a better part-time job, to finish her night school assignment. She no longer thinks or feels or speaks like the girl in the village; she approaches her youthful self across impossible barriers. —You sound like a retard when you speak Spanish! her all-knowing, ever-embarrassed daughter complains. Sweeping her hand over the window, she feels the young girl sliding away even as she struggles to reel her back. She throws down her towel, blinking at the snow. Then a moment's terrifying clarity cracks open her wall-to-wall carpet like a trap door. The chemical odour of her cleaning spray evaporating, she plunges towards the canyon floor.

SEVEN 𝆕

E ach morning, as soon as she wakes, she sits up in her cot, impatient to get out to the highway. The thrice-daily whir of the microbus stokes her brain with possibilities. Every day the fruit in her basket brings her news of unfamiliar names and places. The sergeant takes his leaves in Guayaquil, while the three soldiers take theirs in Quito. She knows that the microbuses begin their race southward in the northern border town of Tulcán. Beyond Tulcán lies Colombia – a foreign country, full of drug addicts and Mafiosos. The name brings back the creak of the maestra's voice in the lattice-walled, dirt-floored school. —Our homeland is the Republic of Ecuador; it borders on Colombia and Peru.—

The thin, despairing teacher never succeeded in investing these names with life. As places, Colombia and Peru seemed far less real than the Heaven and Hell Father Alberto described in his sermons. But her view has begun to change. The soldiers explain to her that due to the threats posed by these countries, Ecuador needs a strong army. The Colombians want to steal the Oriente, Ecuador's foothold in the Amazon, to expand their drug trafficking; the Peruvians attacked Ecuador only a few years ago.

—We must be vigilant, says Gonzalo, the soldier who stared at her from the pillbox the first day. She watches with pride as the soldiers ask passengers carrying Colombian or Peruvian passports to bring their luggage into the main building for a thorough search.

Most of the microbus passengers are Indians from up on the *páramo* who are travelling only a few kilometres. Occasionally there are Peruvians and Ecuadoreans returning from months or years working in a country called Venezuela, where money and good jobs abound. They look exhausted, battered – far from prosperous, despite their new shoes. Nearly every week she sees Otavaleños, the rich Indians from a valley not far south of the village. The Otavaleños travel with huge bundles of weaving which, according to Gonzalo, they sell all over the world. They all wear identical dress: short white breeches, heavy blue ponchos, grey felt hats; they all project the same hardnosed silence. Respecting the Otavaleños' prosperity, the soldiers let them pass unmolested.

Marta does not waste time trying to sell to the Otavaleños. She prefers to tackle the gigantic blond gringos, who carry their belongings on their backs like llamas and bray at each other in a language called *inglés*. The gringos are the most intimidating passengers to approach but the easiest to make money from. Their daunting size and fractured Spanish frighten her until she learns that they are fabulously, carelessly rich. Having recently crossed the border at Tulcán, the southbound gringos remain confused by their fresh wads of *sucres*. They proffer large bills and don't always notice discrepancies in change. Marta rivets their attention with a brilliant smile as she hands them their oranges.

The last microbus of the day stops at the control post just before sunset. (A fourth microbus now passes in the middle of the night, but only the disgraced Hortensia and a clutch of equally desperate women traipse out to meet that one.) Marta lingers at the control post after the evening microbus's departure, watching the sun set and bantering with the soldiers. —I haven't sold very much today, Gonzalo. Do you think that if I stay here another hour a truck might come through?—

—Who knows, Marta? A truck came through at this time last Monday.—

Leaving the control post, she feels bereft. The spattering of the river emphasizes the village's silence. All that drives her down the pebbled slope to the sand-drifted riverbank streets is the pressure to communicate. Each nugget of knowledge – the name of a town, an overheard generalization about the inhabitants of another region, the colour of a foreign passport not glimpsed before – spills out into her supper-table conversation.

Her parents shrug their shoulders at her miracles. —So many things happening up at that control post, Juana says, and meanders on to the subject of potatoes or dust or wind.

Ignacio, stirred to life by an especially vigorous flood of detail, tells the story of how as a young man he used to travel to Quito to buy merchandise for his shop. —Back then, before the truck brought me my order . . . — His journeys to the capital have fused into a single stream of recollection: Marta tires of his repetitions. When she interrupts to tell them about a truck from Ibarra that sagged beneath the weight of an enormous cebú bull, Ignacio turns on her. —Why don't you listen to your parents with respect for a change? A little girl like you has nothing to teach us. You have nothing to teach anyone until you start going to church again.—

After supper she slips out of the house and makes her way through the deepening sand to the edge of the river. The slithering current swirls the white patina of the moonlight. The shaky glimmer of the generator-powered lights at the top of El Lomito deepens the shadow of the church jutting from its hillock at the opposite end of the village. She plunks herself down on the cool sand, morose with shame. The more she learns about other worlds, the poorer and more ignorant her own life appears. Staring up at the canyon walls, she grapples with the idea that this valley is not the only place on earth, not even a self-contained unit: that it is a mere part of something unimaginably huge. She struggles to envisage a role for herself in such an immense world. Her fledgling self-assurance founders at the thought of other highways, other control posts, other languages. Can there be other Martas and Juanas, also? For an instant, she turns her gaze towards the church's silhouette. Father Alberto would counsel her to shut her eyes to the bewilderment of existence. To be meek and humble, to accept God's creation and will. But she cannot retreat from the bewilderment: it forces itself on her unceasingly; it challenges and fascinates her. To become someone new. To become a girl as exciting as the dust-devil variety that comes churning down the highway . . . Father Alberto's assumption that God has curtailed her understanding enrages her. She must understand the strange people she meets at the control post. If God has denied her this ability, then He has created her a cripple.

She drags her fingers through the sand. She knows the name of the emotion that bores through her, sweeping tears before it like scraps of refuse carried on the current

of the river: it is shame. *La vergüenza.* Not shame felt for
a sin of which she can unburden herself through confession, but shame of what she is: poor, ignorant, a peasant,
the daughter of a black woman. Only the racial shame is
not new. Her encounter with the control post has left a
brittle tingling in her cheeks each time she smiles. She
has noticed, too, that since the evenings when the army
construction crew filled her father's shop with their deri-
sive laughter, few nocturnal moans have sounded from her
parents' room. Perhaps they are just growing older, but
she can't escape the thought that shame of their backwardness has blunted their delight in one another's bodies. Or
rather, Ignacio's delight in Juana's body: Juana is too self-
centred to feel bad from comparing herself with anyone
else. The women at the control post have taught Marta
that when a man loses interest in a woman's body the
things that happen at night cease: the man finds another
woman or begins to drink. The thought makes her afraid.
What would she do if Ignacio started drinking?

  She trails home through the chill silence. Dampness
penetrates every ill-aligned block of grey stone that her
father laid, row upon row, under his father's cantankerous
supervision, while Juana, young and long limbed, floated
past in the clear heat of the dry season. Even her grandmother's caustic tale of how her parents married, which
used to enchant her, has been debased into a banal anec-
dote of mindless lust. Did her parents fall in love? Did they
strive to understand their world as she is fighting to make
sense of hers? Or did they respond to one another like
brutish peasants, like the animals that Gonzalo and Eduardo
and Jorge tell her everyone who has not lived in Quito or
Guayaquil is condemned to remain?

The next morning she struggles up El Lomito to the
control post, holding her basket under her arm rather
than balancing it on her head. After the first microbus of
the day has passed, she carries her basket around the side
of the building. The toilet in the front hall is reserved for
the use of microbus passengers and military personnel
(although the three soldiers, like the male passengers, piss
outside); but women who sell fruit must squat against the
windowless side wall of the building. As Marta hoists up
her skirts, bunching them against her stomach, two gaunt
dogs, who use this patch of ground for the same purpose
as the saleswomen, approach her with small, nervous steps.
They draw to a halt and stare, their ears twitching. The
skin pulled bladder-tight over their ribs looks worn as
frayed hanks of old fabric; they are almost hairless. Shame
invades her again. Today she is the youngest and most
successful of the fruit vendors: the girl who is everybody's
friend. In a year or two another girl with more energy and
a brighter smile will wander out to the control post. She
will become one more black woman selling fruit. She will
marry, have a daughter of her own, settle in the village.

She will become more and more like Juana.

The dogs pace closer as she stands up. She hurls a stone
at one of them. They pay no attention, picking their way
towards the side wall of the control post on bone-thin legs
and beginning to sniff. Marta slinks away.

Rounding the corner of the building she comes upon
Gonzalo talking to Jorge. They are standing with their
backs to her; she presses herself against the wall. Their
conversation makes her blush. Jorge boasts about his *amigui-
tas* in Quito who lie on their backs for him the instant he
commands them to.

—These village women! Jorge says. —They look like grandmothers at twenty-five. And we're not even in the village – we're stuck up here with a bunch of black women. *Puras negritas son.*—

—*La Marta es distinta,* Gonzalo says with care. —Marta is different.—

She squeezes her eyes shut, closes her lips and presses them into a taut line. She aches to poke her head around the corner of the building.

—Sure, Jorge says, her skin's not as dark.—

—Yes, she's pretty. *Y es bien simpática.*—

—I don't think she likes me. She never looks at me.—

—That's because you hit her, idiot!—

Deep-voiced Eduardo shouts at Gonzalo and Jorge from the pillbox. They amble across the highway, their voices drifting out of earshot.

Marta withdraws along the wall of the building. The dogs sniff as she rushes past them. She stops, hugging herself. Her basket has become weightless. Marta is different. She won't be condemned to village dust and poverty. Her qualities are evident to all who meet her. She will achieve something magnificent.

EIGHT ⹒

A ll day she studies Gonzalo's movements. His smooth
brown neck, the immaculate line of his jaw, the way
his uniform buttresses his shoulders and clings to
his hips. When he steps close to her to chat, she notices
his square hands, the cuffs of his uniform shirt buttoned
around strong wrists that are neither too thin nor too thick.
As he jokes about an irritable old Chinaman from Quevedo
who passes through on the microbus every Saturday, she
feels part of herself collapsing, spilling towards him. Can
he sense her gratitude? Does he know that in her mind she
has thanked him again and again for his words to Jorge?

That evening she makes a dozen trips to the river. She
fills the old tin vat in the outer room with river water, heats
small pots over the fire until her patience is exhausted. As
soon as Ignacio has finished his supper and left to reopen
the shop for the evening, she undresses and sinks into a
languid bath. Juana watches her with wide, dull eyes. Then,
appearing to lose interest, she drifts out the door into the
night. Marta sinks into the scratchy vat, her brown knees
jutting up in front of her. The tepid water soaks into her
pores. She scrubs and soaps and caresses herself. She
drenches her hair with a pot of water she has set aside,
then reaches for the brush and with a firm motion begins

to pull the spikey teeth through her matted hair. Since childhood she has worn her hair wrapped around her crown and speared in place with a wooden comb. As she unwinds the sodden plaits and brushes them out, she discovers that the dark brown strands are straighter, fuller and much less like a black woman's hair than she has realized. She catches the locks in her fingers and rubs them between her fingertips. Her hair has a wiry quality – it pokes downward rather than gracefully falling – but she could wear it loose if she wished. When she finishes brushing out the heavy brown wings, though, she realizes that her hair is too long, too limp and twisted from being bound about her skull; it hangs in clumps on her neck.

When Juana returns, she says: —Cut my hair, Mamita.—

—There's nothing to cut it with. You can go to Hortensia tomorrow. She cuts men's hair sometimes.—

—I hate Hortensia. Please, Mamita, do it now!—

—We don't have any scissors, girl. What can I cut it with?—

—Shears, she says. —Papi sells shears in the shop.—

Juana shrugs her shoulders and heads out the door. Marta expects to hear an argument erupt from behind the wall. The long silence makes her worry that Juana has forgotten her. A few minutes later, though, she returns, brandishing a pair of broad-bladed shears. —How long?—

Marta runs her hand along an imaginary line a finger's breadth above the base of her neck. Juana measures and snips. The cold backs of the blades kiss Marta's skin. The haircut is over in seconds. She ducks her head under the water and brushes out her hair again. It doesn't seem to be right; she doesn't feel as beautiful as she had hoped. But once she has dried herself and dressed and brushed and towelled her hair, she knows that she has changed.

Peering into her chipped hand mirror, she sees a girl more full-featured than before; her hair thrusts down behind her ears like a stiff, frayed curtain. Against that tousled backdrop, her nose and cheeks have bloomed. Her face is delicate and rounded, its curves gentler than the bulbed features of the *negritas* at the control post.

She turns to Juana. —What do you think, Mami?—

Juana, scrutinizing her, wrinkles her brow. —You look more like Ignacio every day.— She squats down in the lamplit shadow to scrub potatoes for tomorrow's supper.

—I don't look like Papi, Marta says. —I look like a city woman.—

—That's what I said, girl. It's all the same thing.—

She leaves the house in the morning eager to try out an improvisation that occurred to her while she was soaping her body in the vat. Running her hands over her hips, she realized that a body is individual, particular: that it can be presented in different ways that show it off to its advantage or its detriment. Juana may have looked elegant carrying a basket of fruit on her head when she was young, but Marta has always felt self-conscious in this posture. Her body is not lanky and flowing; she stands closer to the ground, more deeply curved. In the hope of making her curves tantalizing she hoists her basket of fruit onto her hip. The stance frees her stride from the complication of upstretched arms. She sways along the gritty street, the lingering morning coolness lulling her mind into leaps of fantasy. She imagines that she is floating above herself, studying the movements of her body. She can almost see herself as Gonzalo sees her. She imagines gestures and expressions that will please him, words and smiles that will draw him forward.

—Look, a strange girl! one of the women at the control post yells. For almost an hour after the departure of the morning microbus, the women taunt her. Between gibes they sidle up to her and coyly run their fingers through her brushed-out locks. When the ruckus dies down, a frigid silence sets in. After Marta out-manoeuvres another woman to sell two guavas to a truck driver, her conciliatory smile falls flat. —Truck drivers like city girls, the other woman sneers. —They know city girls are whores.—

—I'm no city girl. I've never been out of this canyon in my life.—

—Doesn't stop you being a whore. You think you're special because your papi owns the shop.—

—I hate my papi.—

—Doesn't stop you thinking you're special.—

She retreats, muzzled by guilt: she does feel special. But it is the soldiers' praise, not Ignacio's shop, that confirms her certainty of having been singled out. Need makes her miserable. Do the women not recognize the stiff flag of her brushed-out hair as a desperate, inadequate rejoinder to the warm cloth contours of Gonzalo's chest and hips? Then she feels thankful for their blindness. If they knew how defenceless she felt, they would tear her to shreds. Their envious abuse drives her from the bench. She sits down in the dirt. She will endure the sun's glare if that is the price of being special.

Her haircut makes the soldiers stare. Perhaps she has cast a spell on them. Has she inherited the demons Juana used to snare Ignacio? Even Jorge treks over to see her. He inquires in his most formal diction who cut the *señorita's* hair. Her mother? Then her mother must be a hairdresser of great talent. His lightly mocking tone cannot conceal his effort to make amends. She wheels away, scanning the highway for signs of approaching traffic.

Eduardo stumbles over to grunt that if she ever comes to Quito she must visit the Evangelical Church. For the singing, he explains. He knows she would enjoy the singing. He falls silent, shrugs his shoulders and trudges away.

Then Gonzalo strolls over to chat. —It's nice to see something change in this village.— When he walks away a few moments later she knows she has been told that she is beautiful. But he has given her no resonating phrase to cherish and cling to; his compliment has swept past her like a ripple in the brown river.

Watching him climb back into the pillbox and slouch down on the stool, she feels a pang of disappointment. She remembers the first day, when he stared at her over the concrete ledge where foreigners display their passports for examination. She thinks of his reprimand of Jorge's brutality; recollection burnishes his words into a glowing defence of her rights. He would never beat her like Ignacio. He will always treat her with kindness.

In the middle of the afternoon, during a long lull between trucks, she glances up to see him walking towards her. This time, perhaps because the gesture is more deliberate and the audience of soldiers and fruit vendors more greedily attentive, their conversation becomes awkward. The women's giggles tighten his face with tension. As he tramps back to his post, she thinks: everybody knows, he must pay attention to me now. An adversarial tint stains their bond. Having expected to feel borne away by happiness, she is surprised by the defiance that strikes through her. I do have some control over him, she thinks. He can't ignore me now that everybody knows.

On Saturday afternoon, when she half-inadvertently elbows another woman aside in the tumble to be the first to thrust her basket towards the passengers' faces, the others turn on her.

—Runt! Soldier's whore! the whispers hiss. —You're nothing special. The only reason those peasants aren't interested in us is because they're too short to handle us.—

She lashes out with a blind, sobbing swipe, scratches a black cheek and bolts back under the overhang. She plants herself in the middle of the bench. The women, returning from the microbus, mill around in the dust. None dares to challenge her possession of the bench. She slides to her feet and walks away, allowing them to sit down.

She despises them. She climbs the knoll to the control post each morning because Gonzalo will be there: nothing else matters. She burns to know everything about him. Her questions leave him tongue-tied, as though he is flabbergasted by her ability to speak. He tells her about himself in fits and starts. His stiff-jawed utterances, almost always spoken before an audience of fruit sellers, inform her that he is from Quito. His family is large. —Eleven or twelve children, he says. His mother is dead and his father, maimed in a factory accident, lives with one of his older brothers; another older brother, Rodrigo, is rich and lives in *Norte América*. Gonzalo, who plays the guitar, dreams of leaving the army to make his living as a singer.

The women on the bench rock with derision. —A singer! they shout. —*¡Maricón será!* He must be a faggot!— One woman uncorks an ululating gargle whose echoes bounce against the overhang. Her companions break into a discordant chorus.

Marta flinches.

—Shut up! Gonzalo screams, making a threatening jab with his right fist. His face flushes beneath the bill of his military cap; a vein throbs in his neck. —You don't believe me? I'll bring my guitar down into your village tonight and play for you. It'll be the only interesting thing that's happened here in the last thousand years.—

The sergeant appears in the doorway, his brittle-looking arms folded against his chest like crossed sticks. His cadaverous face creases. He blinks into the sunlight. —Back to your post, soldier.—

—Yes, my sergeant.— Gonzalo clicks to attention, salutes, marches across the highway to the pillbox. The stillness of the canyon reimposes itself. The sergeant paces away down the glassed-in corridor. He disappears through a heavy door into the inner rooms of the control post.

Marta seizes her basket and rushes away. She feels no yearning to delay her descent into the village. She doesn't give a damn about the last microbus. She doesn't care about the uniformed boys who will examine the passengers' documents or the women who will claw at each other trying to sell them wrinkled guavas. She wishes she had never in her life carried a basket of fruit up the hill.

Halfway down the dirt path zigzagging into the village, she stops and sits down. He walked away without speaking to me, she thinks. He didn't even try to sneak a glance at me as he was marching back to his post. But what hurts more is that he allowed those horrible women to rattle him: that he flew into a rage and threatened them. She loathes him for his weakness. His name and hers are so inextricably linked that his misbehaviour becomes her foolishness. She is judged by him but cannot control him; he has made no pledge to stand by her. The bitter flavour of a closeness that angers rather than comforts her boils up in her throat again. She feels ferocity crouching in her chest like a jaguar ready to pounce. She longs to grab him by his protruding ears and teach him a lesson.

The wind flails dust against her knees. She stares out at the light brown, clump-spined canyon walls. The memory of Gonzalo stamping across the highway to the pillbox makes her tremble. Why can one stupid soldier's smile change the colours of the day the way the river changes the colours of the valley? She never felt this easily hurt when she was a child.

She scuffs down the path into the village. When she walks in the door of the house and drops her basket of fruit on the table, Juana rolls into an angry alertness, poised on the balls of her feet. —What's going on? Get back up there—there's one more microbus. We need the money!—

—I can't go back, Marta says, sitting down on her cot.

Juana shrugs her shoulders, her long frame drooping. Marta rolls onto her side, burrows beneath the blankets and closes her eyes against the daylight. She will not leave this house or show her face in the village again. She will never return to the control post.

Nine ♫

Y our boyfriend's come to play for us.—
    She wakes to the rise and fall of music, a chorus of
    tattered singing and a celebratory shout. Darkness has
fallen. A cold breeze streams in through the open doorway.
Juana is standing at the foot of her cot, her round black
cheeks motionless. Having announced her news, she turns
and walks out the door.

Marta gets up. In the cold night air she feels startlingly
lucid. She brushes her hair with vigorous, raking strokes,
straightens her skirt and changes into her red blouse.
Looking at herself in her hand mirror, she observes that
the limp scarlet collar darkens the hue of her face. For
once she doesn't care about appearing dark; it won't matter at night.

The wind chills her legs as she steps onto the street. She
rounds the corner of the building; the music grows louder.
The chords resonate, each note striking clear, until the
knotted tension inside her dissolves. A fresh tension snares
her, reeling her along the side wall of the house. Gonzalo's
voice, unbelievably full and powerful after the static-blurred
ditties that sputter from Ignacio's transistor radio, makes
her knees tremble. She had no idea that a man and a

guitar could change the consistency of the air, alter the rhythm of her breathing.

The song rises to a close. The villagers gathered in the shop shout and applaud. Gonzalo thanks them; she imagines him basking in their admiration. She has reached the corner that gives onto the street. The open door of the shop spills a wash of pallid light. She hesitates. Has Gonzalo come down to the village to woo her, or only to quash the mockery of the fruit vendors? Is it love that has brought him here, or pride and vanity? How much does she matter to him?

—You're a very kind audience, his voice rumbles.

He sounds so pompous! Outrage propels her forward to give him a piece of her mind. Even if he comes from Quito and wears a uniform he's only . . .

She shivers to a halt half a dozen paces shy of the shop door. He probably has a girl in Quito, a sophisticated city girl with lighter skin and pretty clothes and respectable parents. Perhaps he has been toying with her all these weeks, sneering privately at her rudely direct peasant questions. She should step into the shop and force him, before the assembled village, to declare his intentions. But of course she can't do it; she would die of shame. And she is not sure she feels attracted to this Gonzalo who is strumming in her father's shop. She wants to marry her Gonzalo from the control post: the Gonzalo who reprimanded Jorge for striking her, not a self-infatuated boy eager to lap up the adulation of all the backward people she despises and longs to flee.

She begins to retreat to her cot, but the music resumes, transfixing her at the corner of the building. She wishes she knew an incantation to make herself invisible. What she would give for a glance through the doorway of the shop!

With careful steps she picks her way into the darkness, rambles out beyond the patch of pale light slanting from the doorway. She turns and stares back towards the shop.

Gonzalo, wearing civilian clothes, sits on the counter, his guitar slung across his knee. His audience crouches on crates and leans against shelves. She makes out Ignacio and Juana, the fruit vendors, the gaunt sergeant (Eduardo and Jorge must be manning the control post this evening). Even the pious women from church are there, although there is no sign of Father Alberto. Gonzalo focuses his gaze on a point above his audience's heads: he seems to be staring towards her. She imagines him scanning the darkness beyond the wavering pool of light in search of her. Lowering his head, he flings himself into a song with a quick, angry beat. *Una canción protesta*, she thinks, straining to discern the sergeant's reaction. The older man's stare remains invincibly glassy-eyed. The song's energy scales through her body, cranking tighter her agonized indecision. Unable either to approach the shop or return to her cot, she hurls herself into a frantic back-and-forth pacing. She hopes that Gonzalo can make out her red blouse waving at him, bright as a bullfighter's cape, from the spot where light merges into shadow. Perhaps, like Juana's stately passes before Ignacio's building site, her activity will lasso his attention, secure his devotion. She struts faster and faster, cutting closer to the doorway of the shop. —Little Marta's gone crazy. She's afraid to go inside to see her soldier.—

Her body turns clammy-cold in the night air. Hortensia, all gangling limbs and yellow teeth, is lolling back from her night shift at the control post, a neighbour at her side.

When they see her, they burst out laughing. Their cackling voices clash with the ringing chords of Gonzalo's guitar. They call out. Bodies shift inside the shop.

Marta runs.

She rushes around to the opposite side of the building and dives into the house. The blankets on her cot are cold. She pulls them over her head, jamming her fingers into her ears to block out the strumming of Gonzalo's guitar. She will lie here until she starves to death. Hortensia will tell everyone that she has gone mad. All Gonzalo cares about is winning the admiration of stupid villagers. He doesn't give a damn about her. Which is fine with Marta, because she doesn't give a damn about him either.

—A girl has to be willing to show a man she's interested if she doesn't want to end up a crazy old spinster, Juana says on Sunday, when she and Ignacio return from church. Marta creeps back to her cot and pulls the rich-smelling alpaca blankets over her head.

Next morning, in the icy darkness, she refuses to be dislodged. —Come on, girl, Juana says. —We all work here. You don't have to talk to the soldiers: just sell the goddamn fruit!—

—I'm not moving.—

Juana's long hand whips around. The smack of palm on cheek drives Marta's head back; the wrench twists the muscles at the top of her spine. She struggles to breathe and discovers that she is sobbing. Juana grabs her by the hair and yanks her off the cot. Her bad leg hits the dirt first: uncoiling agony makes her cry out.

—Well, get up and work, then, Juana says.

Ignacio thrusts the fruit basket into her hands. His hooded stare grows more remote as his heavy, hunched shoulders sag closer to her. —Every *sucre* is important.

They want more money up front for the next shipment
from Quito. If I can't pay, the shop will be half empty next
month.—

She walks out the door, cradling the fruit in front of her.
She can hardly believe that she once tucked the basket
against her hip to make her ass wiggle. Her body feels
denuded, plucked of its charms. She hears the first microbus of the morning whining across the valley floor; she
cannot force herself to rush to catch it. By the time she
scuffles up to the control post the microbus has disappeared into the dry canyon stillness.

—I sold more than any of you, Hortensia is boasting,
swaying her broad shoulders and hips. —See if I'm not
the richest woman here by this evening.—

Marta wobbles to a halt. Her spell has been broken.
Unless she drives Hortensia away instantly, the person she
has become during the past months will vanish.

She feels too stunned to move. A week ago Gonzalo was
hers: she was on the road to marrying him and floating
up off the canyon floor like a decent girl from Quito. Now
she is sinking into the role of a mangy dog of a woman,
an outcast lunatic spinster at whom the village children
will learn to throw stones.

The women spot her standing on the slope. —¡Loca!
¡Loca! ¡Loca!— They are calling her a madwoman already.

Hortensia rushes forward, her long arms wheeling. —
¡Fuera! Get out of here! Crazy runt whore!—

Her cheeks still aching from Juana's slap, Marta clutches
her basket against her stomach. Hortensia's taunting energy makes her feel that she is confronting a vision of her
sleepy-eyed mother gone beserk. She glances towards the
pillbox, but Eduardo's small-boned profile offers her little

hope of protection. Gonzalo, Jorge and the sergeant are nowhere to be seen.

Hortensia's weathered pole of a leg levers up, kicking Marta's fruit basket. The top layer of oranges leaps into the air; three tumble into the dust. The second kick drives Hortensia's bunched, callused toes into Marta's forearm. She drops her basket. Hortensia bowls it over with an adroit slap of her foot. She trips Marta, rolls her onto her back and falls on her in a tumult of hard limbs and dust-laden skirts. Marta goes limp, hoping somehow to withdraw her spirit from the body that has racked her with such misery. Her grandmother would have known an incantation for this. Hortensia slaps her face, pulls her hair, pinches her cheeks. She rams her salt- and grit-tasting palm over Marta's mouth. Bending and shifting her weight to find new targets for attack, she continues to pinch and pummel. In an access of rage that flares up out of her desperation to spare herself further injury, Marta bites Hortensia's hand. She clenches her teeth like a rabid dog, refusing to release the furrow of Hortensia's flesh. If she bites hard enough Hortensia's skin will shear away like torn fabric.

Shrieking, Hortensia beats her on the forehead; her free hand has closed into a fist. Marta releases her bite. Hortensia stumbles away, bawling and moaning.

Her eyes closed, she tries to breathe away her bruises. Pebbles dig into her shoulder blades. She hates herself. She wants to be a madwoman; it is all she feels fit for. Patterns of light scurry over the lids of her squeezed-shut eyes. Far away she hears Eduardo making a grumbled inquiry. Is the little light-skinned girl all right? The dismissals volley back: she's not hurt, she's just crazy. She thinks: I've always been crazy. She deserves her future as the village pariah, the lunatic who never married. She will never leave her cot again. After a few days Juana will stop slapping her. They will bring Father Alberto to pray over her. He will proclaim her driven mad by her refusal to confess, explaining that her overburdened conscience has deranged her. One day she will begin to work again, cleaning the house, picking her way down to the river to fetch buckets of water. She will speak to no one. Life's edges will grow softer. She will stream down a long, gentle slope like rainwater seeping into the earth. Juan, Ana and Isabel's faces await her at the bottom, her grandmother's Quichua incantations warbling in her ears: *Pwwaway*, Martita. *Nuqanchis cieloman risanchis*. All she needs to do to enter that life is to slouch down into the village.

Down into backwardness.

Scorn of the village stirs in her. She no longer believes that she can transform herself into someone above the disdain of decent people; but she remembers thinking that she could. She stumbles to her feet. Her fruit basket lies at her side. Her guavas and bananas have been stolen or squashed underfoot, but she manages to recover some oranges. She dusts off their skins, rubs them until they attain a semblance of their old lustre.

A metallic whining slices through her head. She is not mad: a small truck is racing over the canyon floor. The women shrug themselves to their feet, amble out from under the overhang of the building. Marta steps into the cool, dazzling sunlight. She keeps her back to the women. Silence. Were it not for the sound of the truck's engine, she could hear the scraping of their sandals on the hard earth. Then the hisses come: soft swear-words, accusations that she is a whore, that she has fucked the devil. —*¡Puta! ¡Loca!*—

The truck, when it mounts the rise and chugs to a stop at the control post, is a rusted Isuzu. The three large *mestizo* men squeezed into the cab treat the soldiers with defiance. Marta veers away from the confrontation, gaining a half-step advantage on the other women in making her way towards the passengers sprawled in the truck's small box. Four Indian men are riding on piled sacks of potatoes. Their ponchos folded beneath them as cushions, the men claim that they're broke, that they've just eaten, that only black people eat fruit. One of them, though, allows a bill to show between his gnarled fingers. Marta and Hortensia pounce on him in the same instant. Hortensia pushes her basket forward. Marta slams down her sneaker on Hortensia's bare toes. Hortensia gasps; the other women jostle around her. Elbowing her way forward, Marta exchanges two oranges for the Indian's bill. She rushes back under the overhang of the building and reclaims her place on the bench.

They no longer ostracize her, but she will never again be the favourite. She mingles with the crowd. Her superiority, like Hortensia's tyranny, has been broken down by the village. She knows that life elsewhere would offer her a chance to live better, but how can she get away? What made her think she was good enough to leave? Did she really rush home to share her discoveries with Ignacio and Juana? She tries not to think about it, but she is growing into precisely what she swore she would never become: a shorter repetition of Juana, one more village woman who sells fruit.

Her dreams of escape grow indistinct. News of distant places and miraculous inventions sputters from Ignacio's transistor radio in the evenings (if only the batteries didn't die so often!), but she finds these wonders impossible to visualize. In this village, even a can of Coca-Cola is a luxury.

Eduardo is on duty in the pillbox for most of the week. Hortensia ambles over to ask him where the other two soldiers have gone. Eduardo grunts that they are working with the sergeant in the office. —Working! Hortensia scoffs. —Playing cards, maybe; that I'd believe.—

When traffic appears, Gonzalo and Jorge step promptly out of the building to examine documents and probe the sacks and bundles that the Indians ferry across the canyon floor on their trips from one *páramo* village to another. Marta works to keep two or three vendors or passengers between her and Gonzalo, tries never to get boxed into a position where she must stare him in the face. The closeness would be unbearable. He was deceiving her; it is obvious that he has a *novia* in Quito. She allows herself to glance at him only when he is marching back into the building. The sag of his bottom in his drab uniform trousers, the absurd, strutting way he holds his arms when he walks, like a man who imagines himself always on parade, repel her. She shudders at her stupidity in not having noticed his arrogance.

Yet as Saturday afternoon draws to a close she finds herself longing for him to step out of the building. A week has passed since the evening he brought his guitar to Ignacio's shop. She wishes he would speak to her again – if only, she tells herself, to release her by confirming that he doesn't care about her.

He trots out of the main building, joking with Jorge, to check the last microbus of the day. They snap through the formalities with a briskness that cuts into the fruit vendors' profits. Eduardo, studying the foreigners' passports at the pillbox window, dismisses them instantly. The microbus's big door slides shut, the driver hops in and the passengers roar away. Gonzalo and Jorge walk back to the building. The women, their day's work finished, begin to drift away down the path. Marta trails behind the others.

Before she can clear the overhang of the building, she stops. Far off across the dun-coloured canyon floor, a stitch of silvery light slinks along the edge of the highway. She stares out at the black tarmac squiggle: a filmy ribbon of colour obscures one lane. She can hear no moan of a truck or microbus engine. The mass – it appears too large and shapeless to be a single vehicle – seeps around the coiled bends far below her. No one can run that fast, she thinks, no engine would drive that slowly; since she sees no animals, the apparition cannot be a cart pulled by donkeys. She looks around; the control post is deserted. Eduardo dozes in the pillbox, his peaked cap pointed straight across the road at the wall of the building; the pillbox's windowless sides block his view of the canyon floor.

She must find Gonzalo. She must warn him of the strange creature that is sliding towards their control post.

TEN 9

She squints into the clear, still air. Far out across the valley floor the creature she cannot identify is streaming around a bend in the highway. Bunched squares of gold and blue float on its silvery glimmer. If a waste-laden current of river water were lifted out of its bed, shot through with metallic light and caused to flow along the highway at a fraction of its normal speed, this might be what it would look like. She squints. A tattered train of colour now, the creature slides past the village. It begins to climb El Lomito towards the control post.

Marta races in search of the soldiers. She slams the flat of her hand against the closed front door of the building. —*¡Viene algo!* Something big's coming.— She rushes back to her vantage point. Eduardo, stumbling out of the pill-box, looks where she is pointing and blinks.

—Ay, he mouths. —What has Jesus Christ sent us?—

—Not Jesus Christ: God.— Then, her grandmother's training overriding Father Alberto's first communion lessons: —Praise to Pachamama.—

Eduardo spits into the dust. She ignores him. The creature accelerates as it rushes up the slope towards them. The long streak of colour has broken into pieces. At last she can distinguish the men. Hunkered low, they straddle

thin slivers of light. Unlike any men she has ever seen,
they flaunt bare arms and legs. As they sweep closer, she
makes out their fair skin and wiry, elongated bodies. The
sight of so much exposed flesh makes her want to giggle,
but the rhythmic, purposeful swaying of the men's movements stifles her irreverence. What sort of ordeal or punishment is she witnessing? The men's limber frames pump
as steadily as machines, while the contraptions beneath
them wobble against the steep grade. Sweat plasters the
men's shirts to their deep-chested bodies. Their mounts
pick up speed as they strike the level pavement in front of
the control post. The silent rush of sleek metal, gnarled
muscle, blue shorts and red- and gold-trimmed T-shirts
drives her two involuntary steps back from the highway.
Bicycles! She has never before seen bicycles.

The cyclists speed around the end of the traffic bar. A
second's laboured breathing and the clicking of taut chain
unsettles the air. Then they vanish. Marta steps onto the
blacktop to stare after them. Jorge and the sergeant, stumbling out of the building, salute as the cyclists flash past.

—That's our national team, Eduardo says. —They're
unbeatable. The other countries just give up when they
see an Ecuadorean cyclist coming.—

Marta spins on her heels. The apparition has lifted her
spirits. She has seen strange machines and men's bodies
so scantily clad that shame alone must keep them ped-
dling. Abandoning herself to a buoyant good mood, she
drifts around the corner of the building. Far below, long
canyon shadows stretch to the outskirts of the village.

—Why don't you wait an hour? A truck came through
at this time last week.—

She whirls around. His voice grows deeper, she thinks,
when he sings. He lounges in civilian clothes in the hard

sunlight, his body haphazardly framed by the rectangular wall of the building. He wears bluejeans as crisp as those of any gringo; the word MIAMI crosses the chest of his T-shirt. His face, free from the shadow cast by a military cap, looks more massive and heavy-boned than she remembers; her eyes trace the long hinge of his jaw from earlobe to chin.

A persistent fluttering in her chest keeps her staring at him. Then she turns her gaze towards the ground. —Why should I wait an hour? There won't be anybody to talk to.—

—I'll talk to you.— He takes a step forward, his chest and shoulders warm looking in the sunlight. He stops. His hands hang big and clumsy at his sides. —I could show you the barracks . . . —

He has missed her! She forgets the romantic eloquence she once dreamed of inspiring in him. His nervous solicitude fills her with joy. Despite her efforts to look remote and appraising, she feels an irrepressible smile crease her face. She tries to muffle it, savouring the anguished, bruised expression with which he has delivered his happiness into her hands. The old adversarial closeness rises in her; she vows to wound him for the miserable week he has inflicted on her. Why didn't he visit her house before going to play in the shop on Saturday night? He could have come around on the pretence of greeting Ignacio: everyone would have understood. And why, during this whole unbearable week, has he never offered her a reassuring word?

—You didn't want to talk to me yesterday, she says.

He takes a half-step forward, shrugging his big shoulders as though trying to rally his arms and hands to his own defence. He frowns. She has hurt him. Good. But as his silence continues, guilt and fear of loneliness undermine her triumph. He shuffles his feet, wide and heavy in his canvas running shoes. He darts a glance over his shoulder, takes a step backwards.

—Anyway, she says, how could we talk in the barracks? Eduardo and Jorge will be there.—

—Not tonight. They're on duty.—

—And the sergeant?—

—The sergeant doesn't know anything about anything.— The black down covering his big muscular arms glints in the sunlight as he laughs; the cyclists' bare legs pump before her mind's eye. —He has his own room. And besides, he whispers, he's hardly ever sober.—

She feels herself lolling forward, drawn by the warm pull of his body. If she let herself go, they would melt together in the cool sunlight. The thought makes her burn with shame and excitement. But defiance continues to ride through her. —Why should I come to your old barracks? I should be selling fruit.—

—You shouldn't have to sell fruit, Marta. Your papi owns a shop. He's exploiting you to make a few extra *sucres*.—

Her legs tremble. She doesn't deserve such praise. Yet she thinks: he knows I'm different, nobody else sees it. —Papi doesn't make enough money to pay his suppliers. If I didn't sell fruit, the shop would be empty.—

Her voice cracks as though she were lying. She no longer believes in this phrase. It does not explain anything. Gonzalo feels more familiar than her parents.

They are walking towards the barracks. They cannot look at each other, their pool of conversation grown arid as the canyon floor. She begins to worry about her appearance. Her hair must look ratty and frayed, her brown blouse is dirty. Is he disconcerted by the gap in her teeth when she smiles? Has he noticed how the peeling white-rubber soles of her sneakers slap with each step she takes?

—*Estás en tu casa.* Please feel at home.—

He holds the door for her as he recites the greeting. He follows her into the room and shuts them into the cool, dim stillness. She puts down her basket of fruit next to the door. By the light of four small windows set high in the wall she makes out three identical beds standing in a row on the concrete floor. A large metal box at the end of the room reaches almost to the ceiling. The box has been divided into compartments, like the rich people's family tomb in the village cemetery. Three of the compartments have been shut and locked and labelled; the others hang ajar.

Gonzalo makes for the box, pulls a key out of his pocket and unlocks the compartment labelled G. Rodríguez Roldós.

—This is my locker. Look!— His strong hands haul a block of gleaming black plastic out of the shadow. He passes it to her.

She grips the offering uncertainly, alarmed by its weight.

—It's beautiful, she breathes. —Very, very beautiful.—

—It's a cassette player. I bought it in Quito.— He looks at her from beneath his soft brow. —You put in a cassette and it plays music.—

—What a marvel! she says. The cassette player's weight is making her arms ache. It is much heavier than Ignacio's transistor radio or the hard black belt pouches with ear-phones she has seen the gringos wearing. A cord trails from the back; if the village had electricity, Gonzalo could plug the box in. His casual handling of such a magnificent object daunts her. Would it be all right for her to set it on the floor? No, she decides. She hands the plastic block back to him. —Make it play music.—

—I can't, he says. —The batteries are dead.—

—Oh. It's like Papi's radio.—

—It's this damned sierra. The altitude kills batteries so quickly . . . When I was in the Oriente my batteries lasted for months. I had music every night!—

—You've been to the Oriente?—

—I spent a year in the Oriente. It's pure jungle. The Indians there hardly wear any clothes. The houses have tin roofs – I almost went deaf during the rainy season. The security is very good, not like up here in the sierra. That's because we can drive into the Oriente. The Colombians don't have roads into their Amazon departments; the Peruvians barely have them. They'll never dare attack us in the jungle: they know we'd outmanoeuvre them.—

—I've never been anywhere! she says.

—Poor little thing.— He leans away from her, returning the cassette player to his locker. He seems to be at a loss for a reply. She imagines him sweeping her up in his arms and carrying her out of the village, holding her tight against him until they can see the lights of Quito. What does his tepid response mean? Is he dismissing her as a backward peasant girl? Does he think she's ugly?

She flexes the loose flap of her rubber sole against the concrete floor while he stares into his locker. He turns around, handing her rattling plastic boxes small enough to fit into the palm of her hand. —I've got tons of rock-and-roll: *música norteamericana*. My brother in California sends it to me.—

The gaudy cassette covers blaze with words she can't pronounce, photos of light-skinned men with long hair like the gringos the soldiers call hippies, photos portraying blonde women in almost no clothes. She feels herself blushing. How can Gonzalo spare her a glance after staring at pictures of women like these?

—I've got some great Colombian *cumbias*, too, he says, diving into his locker. His clumsy dignity falls apart in a rush of nervous movement; her confidence returns. When he passes her the *cumbia* cassettes an infantile desire to please twists his broad, plain features. Baffled by his urgency, she accepts the cassettes with a smile. They are less bewitching than the rock-and-roll cassettes: the pictures on the covers are paintings rather than photographs, the words are in Spanish. —They're very pretty.—

—You like *cumbia*?— He hops around her in a clowning dance, making trilling instrumental sounds in his throat. —*Tus besos son como caramelo*, he chants. —*Me hacen llegar al cielo, me hacen hablar con Dios.*—

He lunges towards her, his face growing huge as he tries to dart a kiss onto her cheek.

Before she can think, she is fending off his lurching bulk. She stabs out a hand to catch hold of the lockers. The cassettes clatter to the floor.

—Oh, your music!— She drops to her knees. —I'm so sorry. Will you forgive me?—

—It doesn't matter.— He stands over her, his arms spread wide to receive her.

—Why didn't you talk to me all week? she hears herself shouting. She wants more than anything else in the world to know what his arms would feel like wrapped around her. Where is this frightened anger coming from? —I was so unhappy I almost died.—

No. She cannot believe she has said this. Now he will never touch her. He will go back to Quito and marry a city girl.

—It was because of the sergeant, he says. —*Está muy loco.*
He told me to go down and sing in the village; he said it
would improve the Army's relations with civilians. But I
sang a song about el Ché. I always sing songs about el Ché.
He was a brave man, even if he was a communist. The
sergeant was too drunk to notice at the time, but he
remembered the song when he woke up the next morning. He screamed at us about setting the right example
for civilians. He was furious; he threatened to smash my
guitar. He ordered us to stop talking to people from the
village. Don't worry, Marta, it won't last. He makes these
rules and then he forgets them . . . The son of a bitch!
He's in trouble now. They must have sent him an order
warning that the bicycle team was coming through; I'm
sure we were supposed to be ready to salute them. But he
got drunk and forgot. His superiors are really going to
give it to him! Then he'll forget all the rules he's made
for us. Don't worry, Marta, we can talk . . . —

He stumbles towards her, his hands trailing at his sides.
She eludes him with a deft twist, making her way into the
middle of the concrete floor. The light from the four small
windows has grown muted; in a few minutes night will fall.
Gonzalo scrambles to pick up the *cumbia* cassettes. What
should she do? No one has ever confessed so much to her.
The desperation in his eyes tells her that she possesses the
power to make him happy. She cannot recall the last time
her will affected another person's happiness.

She breaks into a hopping dance on the smooth floor,
flings herself into a rushed pirouette that lifts the hem of
her skirt. As her foot leaves the concrete, she feels the
balanced mass and taper of her body. Gonzalo is staring
at her. His tensed, immobile shoulders look drained of
their muscularity.

Perhaps she has enchanted him, she thinks, swinging into another dizzying pirouette. She cannot believe that she is doing these things. Yet having turned his body limp with attention, she cannot stop moving. She longs to make his devotion go on forever. He will carry her away to Quito and care for her as she deserves to be cared for. He tried to kiss me, she thinks. As long as she keeps dancing, his eyes will never leave her.

ELEVEN

S he can't identify the moment when she starts taking off her clothes. Somewhere between the swishing of her limbs and the rumble of the *cumbia* chorus Gonzalo has begun to sing; her soaring pride turns to hard knowledge: if she wants to secure him as a husband she must do the things that wives do. It is her only way of showing him what she wishes them to become. She drops her crumpled blouse onto the nearest bed, unties the laces of her sneakers, steps out of her ancient skirts. She kicks away her filthy old clothes with a sigh of relief. Her smooth skin, verging on breaking into goosebumps, feels sleeker than any creature that has ever drawn breath in this dusty canyon. Will she appear that way to Gonzalo, who knows Quito and has seen the half-naked Indians of the Oriente? Cool concrete chills the soles of her feet, sending goose-flesh ripples up her thighs, puckering the space between her breasts. She gazes at him. Night is falling. He starts towards her, reaching for her breasts like a man lifting a bottle off a shelf. She feels herself stiffen, rear back from him. Why doesn't he kiss her? He backs off and continues pulling his T-shirt over his head. When he reaches for her again, his hand alights on her hip and guides her towards the middle bed. She paces ahead of him, stretches herself out on her back on the supple mattress. The springiness makes her laugh. She bounces twice, lifts her head to watch him wrestling out of his bluejeans, folding them with hurried military precision. Lowering her head again, she glimpses the rounded shadow of her fruit basket beside the door.

He climbs onto the bed: he is over her, around her. His face hangs in the gloom. His thick arms, two pillars, grow out of the mattress. He shifts his weight onto his knees, freeing his hands to reach again for her breasts. He caresses them with rough squeezing glides that strangle her breathing. She searches for his eyes in the gloom, desperate to discover whether her body pleases him. But he has already rolled his weight back onto his haunches. Squatting at the foot of the mattress, he rearranges her legs, spreading them until her out-turned feet flutter over empty space. He grips his erect penis, misshapen by comparison with the dogs' fleshy crooks she has glimpsed during couplings in the village streets. He brings his whole body forward and for an instant she is certain that what is going to happen is what she wishes to have happen, no matter how much the thought fills her with terror.

He is ripping her in half. Tears start from her eyes as suddenly as if he has cracked her across the shins with a broomhandle. She hears herself shriek. Juana's youthful night-voice eddies back to her: its whimpering cries and demonic yowls. The memory baffles her. She feels no demons inside her, merely panic. Something has gone wrong. If only she could retreat from this moment: step free of her body and run back down the hill to her narrow cot.

Words she does not understand gurgle up in her throat: her grandmother's Quichua incantations, like a river released inside her.

Gonzalo breaks into a sputtering moan and collapses on top of her. His warm weight bears down on her ribs. He shifts his body to enclose her in his arms. She begins to feel more comfortable. The tearing has dulled to an ache; she holds the intruder in her body throttled between her thighs. Darkness has fallen. They lie still for a long time, his body shielding her from the seeping mountain cold.

She recovers her voice. —You haven't kissed me.—

He hoists himself up onto his elbow, studying her through dark, slightly slanted eyes. —The whores don't let us kiss them.—

—I'm not a whore.—

His sleepy eyes give a start. He scrutinizes her face. No one has ever examined her so intently. Staring back at him, she glimpses a scurrying speck of fear. He is only a couple of years older than she is. He runs a hand through her hair, bends forward, kisses her.

After a few minutes, the cold stiffening their limbs, they move under the covers. Gonzalo produces a roll of toilet paper from his locker. He tears off a length of paper, almost luminously white in the darkness, and begins to wipe himself. When he offers her the roll she feels paralyzed by shame for the first time that evening. She looks away from him as she soils the crisp perfection of the squares.

Once they are under the covers, holding each other in their arms, she feels happier than she has ever felt. They cling to one another against the narrowness of the bed and practise kissing. In the heat bred by the slow rubbing together of their limbs, something inside her rises; she thrusts herself against him. He withdraws, frowning at her. Confused by the breathless heave of her respiration, she subdues the demons that have begun to pulse through her body. Gonzalo relaxes into the sag of the mattress, throwing a careless arm around her shoulders.

In his languor he becomes garrulous. He talks about sharing the barracks with Eduardo and Jorge: how they divide up their cigarettes and where they hide their *aguardiente* to stop the sergeant from confiscating and drinking it; how Eduardo cries because he misses his family; how Jorge came back from a leave in Quito with syphilis and had to return to the capital for treatment. They hardly ever fight, although Jorge did bloody Eduardo's nose one night. An isolated posting like this has advantages: more privacy, no barracks bullies to steal your belongings from your locker, less pressure on the sergeant to inflict constant punishment and deprivation on the men to demonstrate his zeal for discipline. The best times are when Gonzalo plays his guitar and they all sing hymns together.

—On Sunday? she says.

—Whenever we feel like it. Whenever the urge to communicate with Jesus Christ enters us. God doesn't just exist on Sunday morning.—

—Father Alberto makes everybody confess their – —

—Priests! All they care about is rules: you say a Hail Mary for doing this, you burn in Hell for doing that. If I spend my whole life following rules I'll never be a famous singer. I want to be a new man. That's why I'm born again.—

She kisses him on the mouth. —Please take me to Quito with you. I'll go anywhere, just take me away from here. When you're a singer . . . when we're married . . . —

—Marta.— He lays a heavy hand on her shoulder.

—What's the matter? she says, squirming around to pull her face higher than his. She glares down at him. —Don't you love me?—

—Of course I love you, but it's not that simple. I can't just leave the Army overnight.—

—Does the Army say you can't get married?—

—No . . . — He shifts towards her. His penis, thickening again, nudges her thigh. The adversarial feeling swirls in her chest. Maybe it will never go away: maybe intimacy is the wrestling of two wills.

He is afraid to marry her; she must marry before she can begin to live.

Rolling onto her side, she runs a caress over his hips. —Yes, he murmurs, like that.—

She keeps caressing him, her hands growing surer, venturing farther, until he sighs and wraps his arms around her.

¶

She dresses when she gets home. Working on the telephone, she goes to the office in bluejeans and sweatshirts. She sits at a table in the main room, survey forms piled before her alongside a broken-backed telephone directory, a mug of ballpoint pens and a styrofoam cup of instant coffee. Her quota is twenty surveys an afternoon, four afternoons a week. She hurries to finish, hand in the forms to the supervisor and catch the bus home. If she gets back first, she changes her blouse and puts on a skirt. The look on his face when he comes in the door to the sight of her presiding over the kitchen in clothes hugging her hard-won trimness glows in her mind through the next day's phoning.

At night, as they doze off to the muted shriek of María's CD player howling up from the basement, he says: —I'd really like to have a child with you.—

—María's almost a woman . . . —

—She'd love it if you had a baby. It might make her less likely to have one herself before she finishes high school.—

—You think so? What if she decided to compete with me? Anyway, we don't have the money. My job barely covers the groceries. And we need yours for the mortgage . . . —

—Don't try to tell me that's the real reason . . . —

She rolls away from him, curling her head into the pillow. The darkness that wraps this house at night is so much better for sleeping than the streetlight-glow that infiltrated the apartments where she used to live.

—Marta . . . — His hands settle on her shoulders.

—I went hungry when I came to this country.— She rolls over and sits up. Against the shrilling of María's music, she stares into the darkness in the direction of her dressing table, the television in the corner, the ajar door of her walk-in closet. —How can I know it won't all disappear tomorrow?—

Part Two

⁊

TWELVE ❧

Crouching barefoot on the cool kitchen floor, she wraps herself in her arms. The light glows orange before her eyes. Kneading each shoulder with the fingers of the opposite hand, she feels cradled and secure. She stares at the ribs of glowing light Rodrigo assured her would grow hot enough to cook potatoes. Heat radiates through the room, yet the orange bars remain inert. Unclasping herself, she reaches for a knife to stoke them into flames.

—Close the door, Gonzalo says. —Rodrigo says it cooks better with the door closed.—

—What does a man know about cooking? You can't cook unless you can see what you're doing. It takes a good fire to make potatoes crisp.— She turns to him. —I cooked potatoes all the time at home.—

He shrugs his shoulders. His hesitation disturbs her. He was the one intrigued by the demented streets the night of their arrival. Marta, protective of María, veered away from the hundreds of hostile faces. The earthquake of the traffic made her shudder. Each car, occupied only by a driver, looked hollow as a ghost. She tugged Gonzalo and Rodrigo back to the apartment. Since then her reluctance to leave Rodrigo's two small rooms has increased. She thought they were moving to a land where people looked like the actors on gringo television shows they watched with Gonzalo's father in Quito: white, rich, eternally grinning. The crippling cold, the throngs of black and brown and Chinese people, the terrifying hippies and the strange, brusque frowns with which shopkeepers serve her, make her tremble. What will happen to them here? How will she raise her daughter?

—Don't try to stoke it, Gonzalo says, it's not a fire.— He cuffs the door shut. —This coffee place . . . —

—A coffee that is not a drink, she says. She laughs in the security of knowing a few words of English, being certain that coffee means *café*. The Sailor, who knows everything, has told them that in Montreal coffee can also be COFI: *Centre d'Orientation et Formation des Immigrants*. The Sailor told Gonzalo that at this coffee, he could be paid a salary for seven months to take language courses.

—Rodrigo didn't go to coffee, Gonzalo says.

—He already spoke English.— If the gringos hadn't changed their immigration law, forcing thousands of Latinos to move to Canada, Rodrigo would still be in California. Marta wishes they had gone to California. There, perhaps, they might have entered the land of pure white gringo modernity that has been hardening inside her as a destination since they boarded the microbus for Quito. Montreal will never be that place; it is too complicated. —We could have gone to California, Gonzalo. If we had gotten into Mexico the way that woman in the church in Quito told us . . . —

—My brother is here. He can receive us in his home – —

—Where we sleep on the kitchen floor.— She waves at their folded bedding stowed in the cavity next to the refrigerator. —At least in Quito we had a bed.—

—It's temporary.— Their eyes meet. She feels her nerve about to give way. His dull-eyed refusal to concede defeat simultaneously maddens and calms her. Yesterday, when his efforts to speak English to the ticket vendor in the Métro were rebuffed by a blast of caustic French, she saw him tremble. Today his stolidness anchors her. Yet behind her hard-earned calm, anxieties creep towards the kitchen's ceiling like trailers of white fog rising from the river to the páramo. As long as they take turns sinking into despair, they will survive. She hugs him, running her fingers through his thickening hair. Their mouths stumble together, their old, tight clutch dashing away the strangeness. They wrestle each other to the floor in a spate of giggles. Only the baby's waking cry prevents them from making love.

Next morning Gonzalo gets up off the kitchen floor with a groan. He stubs his toe against the stove as he pulls on his socks. —Goddammit, today I'm going to start learning English.—

—Wait. I'll come with you.—

—No, Marta. I'm the one who needs to find a job. If you study English, who's going to look after María?—

She shivers as her ambitions turn to guilt. Until her pregnancy she held her own: they married, they moved to Quito once his hitch at the control post expired. Since then, she has lost every battle. She tries to get angry with him, but can't summon up her old fury. At moments like these she realizes that they have become something more complicated than a couple. Since María's birth she has ceased to struggle against Gonzalo and begun to fight *for* her daughter; her own wishes and desires slip between the cracks. Outside, the water freezes rigid, everything is too expensive to buy and the people, colder than the January ice, can't understand each other's languages. She is no

longer able to write Juana and Ignacio letters; she does
not know the words to describe how she is living. Yet in
the most intimate, vital corner of her existence – the family
life that should give her strength to endure the crazy world
outside – she has lost control.

—I want to learn English.—

—Don't be stupid, Marta. I have to get a job. You can
learn when María starts school.—

—But the Sailor says that COFI has a place where they
will look after María while I study . . . —

—The Sailor is mistaken.—

He leaves for COFI alone. When he returns his broad,
soft forehead is creased with perplexity. The coffee counsellors have advised him to learn French.

What language do people speak in Montreal? Opinion
is divided. Rodrigo maintains that French is irrelevant.
English and Spanish are sufficient for his job in the back
room of a bicycle repair shop off Avenue du Mont-Royal;
English movies and TV shows are more interesting. But
the haughty Chilean woman downstairs, who speaks both
languages, claims that only those who speak French find
jobs. They look at one another in confusion. Marta sug-
gests that they consult the Sailor.

The Sailor claims to be Montreal's longest-standing Latino
resident. —When I came here in 1965, I was the only person
in Montreal who spoke Spanish. I used to get so lonely for
the sound of my language that I would hang around the
Immigration office downtown. Today if I want to speak
Spanish I just glance down the Métro platform until I see a
Latino face and say: *'Hombre, ¿hablas castellano?'*—

An Argentine with puffy Germanic cheeks and sad Italian eyes, the Sailor circled the world three times, absorbing fragments of half a dozen languages, before casting up in Montreal. He speaks in a languid Buenos Aires drawl so ludicrously at odds with his brawny build and restless manner that Marta can barely suppress her giggles. The first time they met she mistook him for a gringo trying to speak Spanish. The Sailor is married to Alfonsina, a robust Colombian woman who manages an empanada shop on a sidestreet off Boulevard St-Laurent, a broad street where Marta can do some of her shopping in Spanish. When the Sailor introduced them, Marta vowed not to be taken in by Alfonsina's swaying, large woman's effusiveness: she couldn't imagine a Colombian who wasn't a *mafioso* at heart. She tensed as Alfonsina caressed María, her earrings –hinged bars of gold – clicking at their pivot as she bent forward to flaunt her buckteeth in a smile. Ever since this first meeting, Marta has been wondering whether she can be friends with a *colombiana*.

Gonzalo sits on the floor, strumming at his guitar. His hair covers his ears; as he bends forward to finger out the chords, thick black sprigs swirl over his neck. Ever since he took off his uniform for the last time his body has looked smaller, less taut and tapered than the big-ribcaged torso she nestled against in the control post's barracks.

—You have to choose, Gonzalo. Go to COFI. Learn English or learn French. I don't care which; we need money. I'm not taking María outside again until we've bought her warm clothes.—

—Leave me alone. If we'd stayed at home, I'd have the crowds at my feet by now. It's not my fault if I'm stuck in a country where nobody understands Spanish.—

—I'm calling Alfonsina.—

The Sailor and Alfonsina arrive the next evening. The Sailor wipes his face as though trying to scratch away the hooked scar biting into his cheek next to his right eye. Matching his strides to the heaving of an imaginary deck, he tells them that most people in Montreal speak French, business is in French; but English can be very useful. —You need both languages, but you should learn French first.—

—All my life I've dreamed of learning English, Gonzalo says. —Now I am in *Norte América* and you tell me I must speak *French*? You sound like the coffee counsellors.—

Cuffing him on the shoulder with the heel of his hand, the Sailor persuades him to sign up for seven months of intensive French classes. As she sits in Rodrigo's apartment with María, Marta tries to imagine Gonzalo practising the swallowed resonances she hears around her on the street. She feels proud of him, and jealous of his good luck. As soon as she can find the time, she too will learn to talk like a gringo.

On long, dull afternoons, when she despairs of making Juan, Ana and Isabel appear, she snaps on the television. She props up María before the screen and flips channels in the hope that her daughter will absorb some of the words that come shooting out of the mouths of announcers and hostesses and policeman and passionate couples. Some of the programs are in English, others in French. She often cannot tell which language is which. And even when she can, she remains uncertain which one she should encourage María to learn.

María fills her days. She must be fed and changed and bathed and lulled to sleep. By the time María dozes off at two or three in the afternoon, Marta feels ready to collapse. —Lucky little girl. You're not going to be brought up on dusty potatoes. There's so much food in the shops here! All kinds of food I wouldn't know how to cook, and it's all so expensive we can't afford any of it, but you won't be brought up on potatoes, I promise you that my little daughter . . . —

—Food, María echoed.

—Yes, *food.* Very good. Soon you and I will be chattering away all day while Papi is learning French.— Marta reaches for the expensive little jar with the picture of the gringo baby on the label. As she slides the spoon towards María's lips, María contracts her hands, trying to draw the food closer. She sucks it into her mouth then spits it out, her eyes dancing.

—Bad little girl! Don't do that! Food is very, very expensive here.—

She swabs the smeared morsels off María's face. Their battles over eating and sleeping extend into the evenings. Gonzalo grows jealous.

—You've got the whole day to talk to María, *mi amorcita.* I'm only here at night.—

—Don't you want to talk to her? Don't you miss her all day?—

He grabs María, tossing her about, then settling her on his knee. He bounces her up and down. His leg jerks higher and higher until María's giggles break into sobs and then shrieks. Her snub features knot, wringing out gleaming tears. She is much darker than they expected their child to be, almost a throwback to Juana. —*Mi morenita,* Gonzalo says, in a voice which troubles Marta. Is he ashamed of María's darkness? —*Qué morena mi hijita,* he says, bouncing her harder.

María's sobs grow louder. Gonzalo hands her back to Marta. He trails away, joining Rodrigo in front of the television. Sometimes the two of them go out to a Latino

bar where they can watch Mexican soccer matches broad-
cast, they claim, by satellites whirling through space. Marta,
knowing better than to believe such a *babosada*, feels overcome by anxiety as she wonders what they are really doing.
Lately, though, their friendship has become frayed. Rodrigo
has grown fond of pointing out that they have been sleeping on his kitchen floor for more than four months. They
are ruining his life with their yowling baby, their dirty
clothes and their raucous hymn singing.

—But we never sing when he's home! Marta says to
Gonzalo, later.

—He's just a selfish bastard. He's not really my brother;
he's so much older that we hardly grew up together. I
never knew him until we came here, and now that I know
him I don't like him.— He pauses as the refrigerator kicks
to life; vibrations run through the linoleum beneath their
blankets. —We need our own apartment. Or at least a
room in an apartment. A room wouldn't cost more than
what I'm paying Rodrigo . . . —

—You're paying him rent? You told me . . . —

—I started paying him two months ago. He said it wasn't
fair that we only paid for our food, since we were incon-
veniencing him so much. He complained that he can't
bring girlfriends home any more . . . I had to pay him,
Marta.—

—We're leaving. If he doesn't wish to receive us as
family, we have no place here.—

She feels strong and moral. Her posture weakens when
she realizes that Gonzalo has already made up his mind to
go. Why didn't he tell her when Rodrigo first asked for
money? She is about to lash out at him, but her anger turns
inward: she is concentrating too much on María. The time
she spends focused on her daughter has weakened her

bond with Gonzalo. Or perhaps this is merely what Gonzalo wishes her to feel. Marta does not speak for fear of causing something horrible to happen. Gonzalo starts folding the blankets on the floor.

—We have to leave, Marta says. —Anyway, I'm fed up with sleeping on the floor.—

THIRTEEN ⸿

Do you mind living with *guanacos*?—
—The room's in a zoo?—
The Sailor's laughter makes her cheeks hot. She didn't know that people from El Salvador were called *guanacos*. Why should they be, when there are no *guanacos* in their country? She saw real *guanacos* strutting across the *páramo* high above the village the day that she and Gonzalo rode the microbus to Quito. The Ochoas, with their sturdy, short-legged bodies and slightly slanted eyes, bear a faint resemblance to these beasts. Their four young children, who sleep fanned out among a litter of toys on the carpeted living room floor, howl and scream in the kitchen all evening. The three older children, Cayetano, Ana María and Roque, are named after martyrs of the Salvadorean resistance; the youngest, Brian, is named after the Prime Minister of Canada. After supper the parents retreat to their bedroom, whose sole decoration is a tourist wall hanging that reads *Recuerdo de El Salvador*. The apartment's fourth, windowless room belongs to her and Gonzalo.

They spend the evenings in their room. Through the door they hear the children squabbling over the television while they do their homework. The apartment is near the Jean-Talon Métro station, half an hour's walk north of

where they lived with Rodrigo. Marta misses the area
Alfonsina taught her to call the Plateau Mont-Royal, where
she could visit the empanada shop and hear Spanish spoken on the streets. (—If these French people can keep
their language, Alfonsina says, why can't we do the same?)
She misses the comforting silhouette of the Mountain, now
reduced to a distant hump. Gonzalo, who used to walk to
his classes, has to spend two dollars every day riding the
Métro four stops down and four stops back. Only for the
purpose of worship is their new address more convenient:
Marta has discovered a Latin American evangelical church
in a basement four blocks away.

The makeshift church lies a short walk from the Jean-
Talon Market. The market was built by the Italians, *Señora*
Ochoa tells her. Long plank tables are piled high with
vegetables. She turns a corner and finds herself staring at
the fruit. There are dimpled red apples, smoothly spherical
green apples, peaches and pears, heaped-up bunches of
bananas. No guavas, she thinks. Few oranges. At one stall
she sees fruit heaped up against cans of maple syrup cov-
ered with paintings of the Canadian woods deep in snow.
The women behind the tables, their long hair tied back
with scarves, joke with one another in a language she does
not understand. Though she lingers before their tables,
they ignore her. She wanders closer, until the rounded ends
of the neat little racks on which the apples are stowed brush
against the front of her blouse. The vendor standing nearest heaves herself around and asks Marta a question in what
sounds like French. Marta watches the other women: they
do not rush forward or push each other aside. Marta feels
ashamed of herself. She shakes her head, lowers her gaze
to avoid meeting their eyes, and walks home.

The evening that Gonzalo finishes his course at COFI, *Señora* Ochoa promises to look after María while Marta rides the Métro down to the Plateau Mont-Royal to meet Gonzalo for supper. They eat in what Gonzalo describes as a *bistro*. She follows him nervously through the swinging glass door. What if people laugh at her or make vulgar remarks? What if crazy punks or hippies eat here? What if they are robbed or lose their documents? She offered to celebrate by cooking him a square of steak to accompany his rice and potatoes. He insisted that they eat out; he wants to order her a meal in French.

Biting her lip she watches him read the menu. She feels safe with him again. His shoulders bulge beneath his shirt; his eyes narrow with discernment. I want to feel him on top of me, she thinks. The thought of entertaining such urges amid muted lighting, lush posters and silky *música norteamericana* makes her knees shake.

The waiter arrives. Gonzalo orders: the young man nods his comprehension. Gonzalo points in the direction of her chest and speaks. He is ordering her supper. He is good and capable; he will take care of her. She waits for a current of warmth to wash through her, but her feelings dwindle to an eddy, tainted with anger.

—How do you say 'she wants' in French? she asks.

—*Elle veut.*—

—And how do you say 'I want'?—

—*Je veux*, he says, a little more grudgingly.

—*Je veux*, she repeats. —That's what I'm going to say when the waiter comes back.—

—Marta, it's not necessary.—

—I want to talk, too, Gonzalo.—

—Why do you have to be like this? I wanted everything to be perfect for you tonight.— He stares into his tall glass of beer. The dim light glosses his hair. His face has grown more compact, less powerfully long jawed. It is difficult to believe that this fine-boned figure is the same giant who hoisted her out of the village and promenaded her around the cathedrals and steep cobblestoned streets of Quito with his uniformed arm locked in hers. Even the controlled man who ordered dinner five minutes ago has vanished. —You want to ruin everything. You won't let me play my guitar, you won't let me speak French . . . —

The loft and pitch of his raised voice appalls her. The gringos will take them for peasants. Everyone will know that this is the first time they've eaten in a real restaurant.

She eats her steak, French fries and salad in silence. Gonzalo asks for the bill in French; they ride the Métro home without speaking.

FOURTEEN 𝔤

With the help of his coffee counsellors, Gonzalo finds a job as a salesman. He borrows money from Rodrigo to buy a suit and tie in a shop on the cheap eastern end of Avenue du Mont-Royal. When he returns to the apartment, the guanacos regard him in circumspect silence. The navy blue blazer broadens his shoulders and straightens his spine. He is growing taller again; he can look any gringo in the eye. She longs to take a photograph of him and send it to Juana and Ignacio to convey to them the changes she is unable to explain in her short letters full of preformed phrases whose meanings have dropped away into the gulf separating Montreal from the village.

Next morning he leaves the apartment at eight o'clock. When he comes home in the evening he does not mention his work. Burning to know all he has seen and done, she struggles to remain silent. He will speak about his job when he is ready to do so; it is not her place to pry into men's affairs. During the night he rolls over and clutches her. They make love in choking gasps as their daughter whimpers in her sleep.

She feels more alone when he is away at work than she did when he was studying French. Jealousy rocks her at

the thought of his growing ever more conversant with
details of Montreal life beyond her reach. Why won't he
share his experiences with her? When he buries his face
between her breasts at night his cruising tongue feels thick
with the burden of withheld news.

On Friday he comes home at two o'clock in the afternoon. —They let me off early.—

He hangs up his suit on the lone hanger they have
suspended from a nail, like the nail from which they used
to hang his uniform in their room in Quito. Gonzalo
changes into his jeans and the long-sleeved shirt which,
when doing the wash, she thinks of as his cowboy shirt.
He sits down to twang at his guitar. He plays a song about
Ché Guevara, then lays the guitar flat across his knees and
looks into her face.

—They fired me because I didn't sell any vacuum clean-
ers all week.—

—What?—

María's brown arms, too long for her baby vest, wave in
the air. Autumn's coming, Marta thinks; she's going to
need a sweater.

—It's the fault of those son-of-a-whore coffee counsellors.—

He unslings the sash of his guitar strap from his shoulder and walks out of the room. She follows him into the
uproar of the kitchen. The TV blares, its din barely out-
stripping Roque's grunts as he wrestles Brian to the floor.
Brian kicks out with his tattered hand-me-down sneaker
and strikes the stove a reverberating blow.

—Gonzalo.— She lays her hand on his shoulder. He
shoves her away.

—It's a lie, he says. —The Sailor's a liar, just like all the
rest of them. The gringos tell you everybody speaks French

to trick you into learning an irrelevant language so they can keep all the good jobs for themselves.—

All week he has knocked on the front doors of palace-like houses. Each time the door opened, he began his courteous, memorized French sales pitch. His words were greeted with uncomprehending smiles. Again and again, as the door slid shut, he heard the polite murmur: "Sorry, I don't speak French."

—In the whole week I only met a couple of people who spoke French.—

—In the warehouse, *Señor* Ochoa says, everything is in French. At school the children speak French.—

—I walked for five days through Côte St-Luc and Westmount – —

—Côte St-Luc and Westmount! Those are English *barrios.* Why didn't you ask them to send you to a different part of the city?—

Señor Ochoa growls at his children to turn down the television.

As they return to their room, Gonzalo looks stricken.
—It's not your fault, she says. —How could you have known? You can't be expected to know things like that. You were just trying to do a good job, I know you were, Gonzalo.—

She hugs him. He shrugs himself clear of her embrace. He starts to sit at home all day playing his guitar. They sing hymns and some of the old songs about revolution, which still console Gonzalo. They subsist on packets of noodles sold with a sack of instant cheese sauce attached. Marta would prefer to cook potatoes or rice, but Gonzalo no longer wishes to eat either. —We're not living in your village any more. We're not peasants, are we?—

—I don't know who we are.—

The noodles, which cook quickly, enable her to get in and out of the kitchen fast enough to avoid angering *Señora* Ochoa. Once every couple of days *Señora* Ochoa knocks on the door and tells her she has a telephone call. Gonzalo takes the receiver, listens for a moment, then murmurs: —*No está.*—
—Who is it? she asks. —Why did you say I wasn't here?—
—Wrong number.—
He picks up his guitar. She sits down next to him on the foam pad that serves as bed and couch. —You have to get a job, Gonzalo.—
—How can I find a job when they forced me to learn a useless language?—
He disappears for hours. When he returns his body looks dark and shrunken. He strums his guitar with a sullen fury and forces himself on her at night with an abruptness that makes her want to cry. She buckles her lips, determined not to utter a sound. María will not be woken at night as she was woken as a little girl.

Then he loses interest in her body. He tells her she is dumpy and slack. Her hands shaking, she traces the soft swells of her stomach and hips. It's true she has put on weight since María's birth. Her breasts are no longer those of a young girl. Her extra bulk dismays her. How can she be getting fat when they have so little to eat? Does Gonzalo appear smaller to her because she has grown larger?

One afternoon as she is settling María on the foam pad for her afternoon nap, the Ochoas walk into the room. They survey her boxes of folded clothes and hoarded plastic shopping bags. Gonzalo's suit, hanging against the wall, stands out as the only decoration. *Señor* Ochoa, always less brusque than his wife, meets her eyes. —You know the rent was due yesterday?—

She looks down at María's dozing form. —Talk to Gonzalo.—

The Ochoas retreat to the kitchen. *Señor* Ochoa, who works an early shift at the warehouse, usually goes to bed at nine. Tonight he waits in the kitchen until nine-thirty. Gonzalo comes in the door just as *Señor* Ochoa is stumbling towards the bedroom. The finicky precision of Gonzalo's step tells her that he has been drinking. He has been with Rodrigo. They are becoming *compañeros* again, spinning out drunken fantasies when they should be trying to find Gonzalo a job. The thought of them together, beyond her reach, makes her feel abandoned and desperate; the sight of Gonzalo's tipsy gait looses a scrambling panic in her chest. What will become of her if he degenerates into one of the drunks who lurches around Parc Jeanne-Mance annoying decent families who come out to watch Latino soccer games on summer weekend afternoons? What will happen to María? She jumps to her feet. She must bring herself as close to him as she was before María's birth. She must defeat this strangeness that is pushing them apart. Peeping around the ajar door, she watches *Señor* Ochoa accost Gonzalo with laboured bonhomie. Warmth doesn't flow naturally in these *guanacos*; they have to pump it up from the depths of their humourless, hard-working souls. *Señor* Ochoa lays his arm along the slackened mantle of Gonzalo's shoulders. It confuses her to observe that the short, squat *guanaco* is the same height as Gonzalo.

Señor Ochoa pulls Gonzalo close to him. —You have to get a job to pay the rent, brother.— He pauses. Then the scandalous words pass his lips: —Isn't that right, *coño?*—

Marta recoils as Gonzalo pivots, his long hair swishing up at the ends, and punches *Señor* Ochoa in the side of the face. He is too drunk to put any weight behind the blow. *Señor* Ochoa stumbles back a step, blinking in amazement.

He straightens up, thrusting his body forward. —Are you out of your mind?—

What sort of reaction did he expect to that filthy word? Marta feels filled with a flushed, bitter loyalty. She steps forward, standing at her husband's side.

Señor Ochoa shouts for his wife. Before she can bundle herself out of the bedroom, the children crowd into the kitchen. They rake Marta with hostile stares.

—Go back to bed, Marta says, waving the children away. They don't budge. She appeals to *Señor* Ochoa, but the men have fallen silent.

Señora Ochoa flings herself at Marta, her flyaway pink dressing gown flailing around her. She is bigger than any of them; she is the largest person in the apartment. —Your husband is a drunken thug! My husband takes you in off the street and your husband turns around and hits him!—

—Your husband insulted my husband, Marta says. —*Va diciendo groserías.*—

—I didn't insult him, *Señor* Ochoa says. —In El Salvador a man calls his buddies *coño.*—

But this is no longer the point. Marta feels herself withdrawing, her fingers seeking the support of the back of a chair. The men have reassumed control, stifling the conflict, but they have done so in a roughhouse masculine way that leaves everyone's resentments alive and aching. She turns away, closing the door of the back room to prevent their raised voices from waking María. *Señora* Ochoa herds her children into the living room. They jostle, refusing to return to their blankets on the floor.

—You're always disrupting us, *Señor* Ochoa mutters. —You and your rowdy singing.—

Gonzalo blinks. —I must express my . . . my personal relationship . . . with Jesus Christ . . . —

Señora Ochoa crosses herself. —In the name of my dead children . . . —

—In El Salvador, *Señor* Ochoa says, his eye sockets yawning above his plaid shirt, they convert the death squads to Evangelical Protestantism to make them better killers.—

Marta feels pity for the Ochoas. She wavers, uncertain what to say.

—I'll pay you the rent, Gonzalo says. He sounds exhausted; he has forgotten to shave. —I'll pay you the rent, but I won't spend another night beneath your roof.—

Before she can move or speak, he has stumbled into the back room and returned brandishing a wad of cash. María has begun to cry. Marta hurries to pick her up.

—You stay here or these *guanacos* will give the room to somebody else, he shouts, as she leans over her daughter in the dark. —I'm going to spend the night with Rodrigo.—

The door slams. She rushes out into the kitchen, heading for the corridor. By the time she reaches the beige-tiled passage, he has disappeared. She hears the comfortable thump of the elevator doors closing. María's cries rise above the wrangling behind her.

—Come and calm your little girl, *Señora* Ochoa says, leaning into the corridor. —My husband has to leave early for work. My children have to get up for school.—

—But Gonzalo, Marta says. —I have to talk to him.—

Señora Ochoa grips the collar of her sagging dressing gown. —Just leave him alone for the night. Don't you know that's the only way to deal with them sometimes?—

Marta returns to the back room and sinks onto the foam pad. She holds María close to her until the little girl's breathing grows even and steady, her clenched brown fists dropping open. Gonzalo does not wish to be with her tonight. That is all she can think about; that is all that matters. The women washing clothes at the riverbank say that the things that happen at night cease when the man gets bored with the woman's body; the man begins to drink or finds another woman. *Pachamama,* she chants, holding the words inside her head in order not to wake María, *please let it be only his brother he's drinking with.*

FIFTEEN ꝯ

Afterwards the line between being with Gonzalo and being alone fogs over. She can no longer remember when she stopped expecting him to arrive in the evening – when she started taking his absences for granted. He mails in the rent money, but never comes home.

One day Alfonsina calls her. —I've been phoning you for weeks but your bastard husband says you're not home and hangs up.— Marta remains silent; it is *her* business to criticize Gonzalo. —Don't defend him, Marta, Alfonsina says. —The Sailor met him in the Métro. I'm calling to tell you what he's doing.—

Gonzalo and Rodrigo have formed a folk group. They play *charangos* and *rondadores* for the dollars tossed by tourists strolling over the red bricks of Rue Prince-Arthur; in cool weather they take refuge in Métro stations to serenade commuters. They tell inquisitive listeners that they are from Chile or El Salvador, countries whose political oppression sympathetic gringos respect. According to the Sailor, Alfonsina says, Gonzalo is sporting a mustache and wearing a poncho.

—A poncho! Marta says. —Like an Indian from the *páramo*! And he used to look so handsome in his uniform.—

If only she could speak to him. She knows she could persuade him to come home. She searches for him in vain at the church near the Jean-Talon Métro station. Her despair sighs out of her in the hymns she moans standing shoulder to shoulder with Guatemalans and *guanacos* who, like her, have been born again as new people equal to the challenge of the city. Why does Gonzalo no longer come to church? If she saw him she would remind him of the dreams that bore them out of the village, sustained them in Quito and buoyed them to join his brother in *Norte América*. She would show him his daughter's face longing for a father's firm attention. She sobs her bitterness into the crumpled pillow on the foam pad. She cannot help it if María shudders until she, too, begins to wail. Having no one else to turn to, she clasps her hands around her daughter's shoulders. —Why did we come here, *hijita*? Why has this place made Papi so stupid?—

Does he have another woman? Alfonsina claims not to know. Marta pinches and pulls at her stomach as she undresses, hating the too-full flesh that has wearied him into leaving. How can she counter his disappearance? She coaxed him into marrying; he insisted that in Quito they would live with his family; she sowed the idea of emigration in his mind, but he had decreed their destination. Every impulse that has flickered in her veins since the first time she carried her basket of fruit to the control post has been tested against his resistance. Without him, it exhausts her to walk to the grocery store to buy noodles.

During the days that she and María lie in the darkness the warm, forgiving face of Jesus Christ, whom she learned to love holding Gonzalo's hand in his church in Quito, dwindles inexorably from her mind's eye. In the absence of Gonzalo's fingers and tongue caressing and teasing her between the sheets at night, Jesus's lustre fades. She struggles to recapture the enlarging magic of those services in Quito, when the heat of Gonzalo's body pressing into hers told her that she had put the village behind her forever. She drags herself to the grated, guarded basement with the bright blue lettering next to the door three, four, five times a week. But Jesus Christ obstinately keeps his distance. Juan, Ana and Isabel, meanwhile, steal into her room. Lying on her pad she spins around the dusty cemetery with them. They dodge Father Alberto and flee her grandmother's cackling complaints. She sends María out to play with them. They make healthier companions than the rough *guanaco* children.

One day the *guanacos* walk into the room, turn on the light and announce that another month's rent has come due. This time Gonzalo has not mailed them an envelope of twenty-dollar bills. Her brother and sisters recede into the same inaccessible well as Jesus Christ. She sits alone on the mattress, bewildered by the *guanacos'* demands and unable to believe that Gonzalo is not there to look after her.

—We need the money, *Señora* Ochoa says. —If we don't pay the concierge we'll all be out on the street together.—

She goes to look for work. The only job she can find, through a friend of *Señora* Ochoa's, is in a garment factory. The cramped, rattling factory floor swarms with tall black women who try to speak to her in a language that might be French. They mistake her for a woman from their island; the boss, who speaks English, makes the same mistake. He has to resort to a bedraggled-looking Mexican woman to explain to her how the factory works. First, the Mexican woman says, she must earn her job. She can do this by working productively for three weeks. If at the end of three weeks the boss is satisfied with her work, they will begin to pay her. From then on she will earn four dollars fifty cents an hour.

For three weeks she bends over a sewing machine frantically stitching the seams of gaudy shirts. Her head reels with the heat and the noise and the incomprehensible banter of the tall black women. Sometimes as she is rushing to complete a seam she glances up at the women, afraid that they may resent her intrusion into their factory. But they do not kick out at her, compete with her for fabric or try to sabotage her work. Nor do they greet or mother her. They pay her no attention; they are all working too hard to care whether she becomes a permanent feature of their world. Anxiety about María, spending the days alone with *Señora* Ochoa and her children, makes Marta's fingers wobble against the slippery synthetic of the shirts. Her sewing machine cuts jiggling lines along cuffs, leaves threads dangling from pockets. At the end of the third week the boss dismisses her without pay. She returns to *Señora* Ochoa in a rage. —They cheated me. You can't throw me out now. You have to let me stay.—

—You'll be two months behind by next week. How are we supposed to buy food for our children?— *Señora* Ochoa closes and stacks splayed schoolbooks as she clears the kitchen table for supper. —Haven't you learned that it's not worth the trouble for a woman to work in this country? It's different for the men. They can go into a warehouse and earn seven or eight dollars an hour. But a woman is only paid four dollars or four-fifty for sewing or packing clothes. By the time you've bought your bus pass and made your lunches and found someone to look after your children there's nothing left. If you had told me at home that I could earn four dollars and fifty cents in an hour! . . .

But's it's so pitifully little when everything costs so much. What a crazy country: so much wealth and no way to get rich.—

Brian, wrestling María to the floor, shouts: —¡*Negrita sucia*! Dirty little black girl!—

Marta seizes her daughter's shoulders and hauls her against her side. María staggers to her feet, tears smearing her cheeks. She is growing taller; she will turn two after Christmas. Her legs unfold to a narrow, bowed and dimpled length. Her eyes are glassy in bruised bafflement. Before she can burst into sobs, Marta hurries her into the back room. —Don't worry, *hijita*. We won't be living here much longer.—

—Are we going to live with Papi?—

The question takes her aback. —I don't know where we're going, she says, staring at the windowless walls.

SIXTEEN ꝼ

Alfonsina saves her. —You must sign up for language courses.— The government will pay to keep her alive while she masters one of Canada's two official languages. She can claim the same benefit that Gonzalo received. She balks, unable to believe that such tales can be true. Why will people she has never met give her money to study? It is understandable with a man, who can go out and earn a good wage, but will they really support a woman? She remembers her early battles with Gonzalo over language courses with unease. She knew so little then about life in Montreal. Now she recognizes how difficult it is to get what you want in this city. Every day her possibilities feel more restricted. What will happen if she isn't intelligent enough to learn another language? She thinks of the bedraggled Mexican woman who interpreted for her in the factory. If she was able to learn another language, so can I. Yet her confidence falters. Shut up in her room, she spins through the cemetery at the crest of the knoll with Juan, Ana and Isabel.

Alfonsina and the Sailor haul her out of the apartment. They parade her through government offices, answer questions on her behalf. As they wait in the outer office of the last official, the Sailor drums his heels against the floor.

—*¡Imbéciles! Ché,* why can't they get a move-on?— He gets
to his feet.

—You're not going anywhere.— Alfonsina grabs his
jacket. —We're here to help Marta!—

—I've had enough! he says, thrusting Alfonsina away,
just as a soft voice calls Marta's number. She remembers
her first encounter with officials sitting behind desks,
when Gonzalo and his father took her to apply for a
passport in Quito. In the village, her surname had been
silted over like an untrod path. She felt unnatural pre-
senting herself as Marta López; her married name, Marta
López de Rodríguez, typed out on her passport applica-
tion, was a responsibility too heavy to bear. She watches
Alfonsina push a form towards her while the gringo official fingers a cigarette lighter and prods a stick of chewing
gum into his mouth. Roused from her famished stupor
by his patter of inquiries, she interrupts him as he is about
to enrol her in French courses. —I want to study English.—

Silence. The Sailor throws up his hands, wipes his scar
and gets to his feet. Alfonsina leans forward in her chair.
The gringo mumbles that as an adult she has the right to
study the official language of her choice. The morning
that she finds her way to the language school, she feels
that she has won a victory.

There are two other Latinos in her class. Restless, flirtatious young men from Honduras, they cease speaking
to her the instant she tells them that she is married. They
murmur to each other; they address her as *Señora.* Unable
to communicate with the other students, most of whom
come from countries she's never heard of, she falls into a
nervous, distracted silence. In order to pay back the two
months' rent she owes the Ochoas, she has limited their
food consumption to two small packets of noodles a day.

Each trip to the shop has become agonizing. Why do they heap such piles of delicacies on the shelves when no one she knows can afford them? Hunger heightens the unreality induced by the circle of strange faces surrounding her beneath glaring classroom lights as she struggles to form the sounds that animate movies and rock songs.

Her second week in the class the teacher asks her to act out the role of a tourist visiting New York. Tourists, she thinks: gigantic blond people who unfold their long legs from the back seat of the microbus. How can she pretend to command their easy wealth, their effortless knowledge? If she tried she would make a fool of herself, or perhaps utter words which would offend the boyish gringo teacher. She falters, sits down without speaking. Is it necessary to stop being yourself to learn another language? Is that why Gonzalo, having learned French, renounced his family? If she could express herself better, she would tell the teacher how frustrated the exercise makes her feel. He is not doing his job. He should teach them, rather than sitting back and demanding that they humiliate themselves.

Her third week at the school the teacher, through a flurry of laboured explanations, conveys to them that he wishes them to act out the roles of survivors of a shipwreck floating in an overcrowded lifeboat. Each student is assigned an identity and asked to present the reasons why he or she does not deserve to be thrown overboard. Marta draws her card: *You are a 25-year-old research scientist who is working on a cure for cancer. You are also a gay-rights activist.* The teacher patiently explains the meaning and implications of each identity. When he describes the activities of a "gay-rights activist", Marta feels mortified. Hot shame sears her face. She must have misunderstood. The whole class is staring at her; the Honduran boys are leaning away from her in their seats.

"I will jump off the boat," she volunteers. "I will kill myself."

"No," the teacher says. "You are a gay-rights *activist.* You are proud of your lifestyle –"

"I will kill myself. My family will be *tan avergonzada de mí.*" She will never tell anyone about this exercise. Never. If the *guanacos* find out that she has been saying such things, they will kick her out of the apartment. She will never be able to look Alfonsina in the face again.

"If you kill yourself," the teacher says, "there's no role-play. You must argue for the point of view of – "

—He thinks I'm a disgraceful degenerate, she says to the Honduran boys, hoping to stifle their shocked sneers. —Any decent person who found out he was like that would kill himself.—

—Not in this country, one of the boys replies. —Here everybody is crazy.—

"We have to respect each other's values," the teacher says. "You must imagine what it *feels like* to be a gay-rights activist."

"I will kill myself." —*No permito que este muchacho me diga groserías.* I won't allow this boy to speak to me with such outrageous rudeness.—

Next morning she does not return to the school.

She hides in her room. All day she watches María scamper through the wind-swirled sand of the cemetery with Juan, Ana and Isabel. The guanacos do not ask her why she has stopped going to English classes. At the end of the month, when the government cheque fails to arrive, she flies to Alfonsina's shop in a panic. Alfonsina and the Sailor parade her through more government offices, answer more questions on her behalf. At the end of an exhausting afternoon she is told that the payments will be resumed on the condition that she go to COFI to study French.

The teachers at COFI grimace when her efforts to speak French issue in mangled English. Unlike the boy at the English school, they are not afraid of their own knowledge: they lead the class through verb drills and dictations; rather than preaching moral laxity, they explain that Quebec is a French-speaking nation and that her role as a néo-Québécoise is to integrate into the values and culture of the Québécois people. Grateful to be welcomed at last – COFI even provides a room of kind young women who look after María during the day – Marta practises French irregular verbs late into the evening. And to think that two weeks ago she did not know what a verb was! English, in its formlessness, fades from her memory. At night all her acquired tongues peel away, stripping her mind to an attentiveness receptive to her grandmother's cries: *Pwwaway, Martita! Nuqanchis cieloman risanchis. Apurakuy! Kunitan risanchis.* Fly, little Marta! We are going to heaven. Hurry! We're leaving right now.

She wakes in the mornings with her stomach churning and her head light. She rocks María to placate the moans hunger wrings from her round, woebegone face. The first words to stumble from Marta's lips are in French. —*Lève-toi, ma petite.*—

—When Papi comes back, María asks, will he bring us food?—

The question reassures Marta. Alarm grips her when her daughter subsides into long, dull silences. Uncertain whether María is conserving her energy by not speaking or simply is not learning to talk as other children do, she keeps on the lookout for the smallest sign of backwardness.

María will never have to haul buckets of water from the river; she will never have to submit to having lice picked from her scalp at the end of the day. But she is suffering from the absence of her father, from not growing up in a normal family – deprivations that Marta was spared. Deprivations from which Juana, with the curious indolent strength Marta never appreciated at the time, shielded her. María is learning the indignity of groaning with pangs of hunger in the midst of plenty. Marta feels herself going wild with anguish when she thinks that her determination to provide her daughter with a better life has merely subjected her to different forms of hardship.

She stares at fruit on stalls in the Jean-Talon Market: bananas, apples, pears. She used to receive so few Ecuadorean *sucres* for each orange or guava she sold, and here they demand so many Canadian dollars for the fruit they must bring from her country and others like it. She cannot bring herself to pay such prices. She longs to have back the guavas that Hortensia flung away. She concentrates as hard as she can, hoping to summon up the fruit through time and space to soothe her daughter.

She finds a *pâtisserie* which sets out stale bread on a rack inside the door. When she has enough money she slips out of the room while María is sleeping and grabs one of the bags containing half a dozen stale croissants, a spar of chocolate baked into each one, that sell for $1.89. She rushes back to the apartment, her fingers quivering. They tear the transparent plastic bag and stuff croissants into their mouths, saliva welling over their gums before they can take their first bites. Sodden, the bread becomes easy to masticate; but an hour later the small chocolate spars swallowed whole begin to scrape against the walls of her swollen stomach. María writhes. Her tiny, purplish fingers purse over her belly. The longer they subsist on noodles, the greater becomes their craving for sugar; by noon María is asking when they can eat more croissants.

As her French improves, Marta risks asking each of her teachers at COFI if they recall her husband. A small Ecuadorean man who carries himself like a soldier? They shake their heads; they meet so many foreigners. She persists. They haven't seen him? They don't know where he might be? No, they say, their faces blank. No one has seen her husband.

SEVENTEEN ❦

When the weather grows warmer, she takes María to Parc Lafontaine on Saturday afternoon. Among the joggers and cyclists and lovers, the upper pond with its spurting fountain and the lower pond swirling with colourful pedal boats, she finds sufficient peace and quiet to relax. —Lucky little girl! she exclaims, when María returns from a dash in pursuit of one of the not-quite-tame pigeons strutting along the slope. —You're never going to play in dust and dirt, are you?—

María smiles and totters off. Marta watches her with a lazy, unconcerned gaze while revelling in the strong, warm sunlight and the languid bustle of city dwellers enjoying themselves on a weekend afternoon. If she is not quite part of this idyllic scene – her husband has vanished, her French remains imperfect, problems of money and food continue to exhaust her – she can still feel a trembling exhilaration at the thought that María might one day meld into the luxurious background of the park's two ponds. Nothing else matters. Gonzalo's treachery is inconsequential. It will take more than Gonzalo to derail her plans.

—Play with me, Mami! María calls. She tags Marta and scampers away on bare feet. Marta sprints after her, catching her beneath the armpits. They tumble together into the grass. Solitary men and elderly couples turn their heads as María squeals. The pairs of embraced lovers barely stir. Marta, suddenly conscious of creating a disturbance – will these sedate gringos think her primitive? – calms her daughter and retreats into the shade of a poplar tree.

A stocky man wearing glasses is watching her.

She hauls María against her chest. Seagulls scream overhead. When she releases María, the girl darts down the slope towards the stranger. The man is smiling at her. She avoids his scrutiny, keeping her eyes trained on María's zigzagging course.

María flings herself in a plunging dive at a stiff-legged, brown-breasted pigeon. With a flurry of flashing bare feet, she trips, falling at the man's side as the bird flutters upward. Her cries skim across the still water of the pond.

Marta hurries forward. Perching María on her knee, she wipes away the tears from her clenched cheeks. She coos in her ear, promising her that when they get home she can play with Juan, Ana and Isabel.

—How old is she?—

The deep rumble of his voice makes her jump. Her attention fixed on her daughter, she has ignored his closeness. She raises her head. The collar of his shirt, slewed to one side, lies splayed open against the heat. Sweat beads his throat below the jut of his Adam's apple. His receding hairline is counterbalanced by the silvery-streaked unkempt ruff of his beard.

—She is two and a half years old, Marta says.

He looks her up and down in the bruised, slightly defensive way in which her COFI teachers often regard her. —You're Haitian?—

She shakes her head. —I come from Ecuador.—

He looks baffled. Another one who has never heard of her country! Why doesn't she just present herself as Mexican or Chilean – as a native of a country people hear about on the news? The man's expression clears. Incisive brown eyes gleam from the amid the dry cross-hatching of his wrinkles. His fingers brush the frames of his glasses. —You had her down there?—

María's head swivels. She delights in being talked about. Her effortless comprehension of French, gleaned from the *guanaco* children and the women who look after her at COFI, stymies Marta. Her tiny, vulnerable daughter should not be standing in judgement over *her* command of the language of daily speech. She tries to think how to tell this man about María.

—Why did you come here?—

The eternal question. *Why couldn't you stay at home in your own country where you belong?*

—I thought it would be easier to find food for her here.—

—You don't have food in your country?—

—We have potatoes and rice and rolls and oranges and bananas and guava fruit. Here you have everything, but it is too expensive so we must eat noodles.— She pauses. Made nervous by his puzzled stare, she hears herself say: —I am poor. I was poor at home. You don't stop being poor just because you change countries.— He looks taken aback. In an effort to guide the conversation onto less harsh terrain, she waves at María. —She understands French perfectly. They speak French to her in daycare and some-times she uses English words because the children all watch English television together. But I want her to re-member Spanish to speak to me. The three languages are becoming too much for her. She mixes up the words. So I take her to church to speak Spanish.—

—Yes, he says, there are Québécois priests who speak Spanish.—

—I'll never take her to a priest. Never.— She flounders, anger banishing her command of French. Does he take her for a prissy old Latin American grandmother obsessed with never missing a Mass? She's no *abuelita*. She watches the fountain: crystal-like bursts of water glint white against the shingled curtain of leaves. Sparely clad cyclists flash past and she no longer concedes them a glance; immersed in the city, she will not tolerate this overbearing gringo writing her off as a peasant.

—Priests tell you to be weak and obedient, she says. —If you obey them, everyone exploits you.—

—Yes!— To her amazement, his eyes widen in agreement. —When I was a boy I refused to go to church. The church used to control everything in Quebec: they kept us weak so that the *Anglais* could rule us.—

—*¡Sí! ¡Así es!* Your relationship with a priest doesn't matter. What matters is your personal relationship with Jesus Christ. In the Evangelical Church of God we are all individuals. The missionaries are very well dressed, they come from Alabama and Alberta and they all speak Spanish. I take my daughter there on Sundays because I know she will conserve her culture. There are only Latino children at my church. They give them Sunday school classes in Spanish. The children speak Spanish to each other. That way I know she won't forget her language.—

The man shakes his head. He looks perturbed. What has she said wrong? She thought they understood each other.

—You can't preserve a language in church, he says.
—We tried that in the 1950s. Anyway, you're in Quebec
now; your children should speak French.—

She clutches at a twist of grass, terrified of offending
him. When was the last time a man spoke to her on equal
terms? —I want my daughter to understand me, she murmurs, bowing her head.

María springs to her feet and pelts up the slope in the
direction of one of the brown-breasted pigeons. She dives;
the pigeon eludes her. The man stirs, a wry smile twisting
his narrow mouth.

—What's your daughter's name?—

—María.— Feeling bidden to speak, she shifts on the
grass, straightening her legs before her. Noticing his eyes
tracking the sweep of her knees and ankles, she stiffens.
—I was supposed to be called María. But the priest wrote
my name as Marta and my parents were afraid he would
send them to Hell if they called me María. They called my
sisters and my brother by their real names. But my real
name is not my real name.—

—Your name is Marta?—

—Yes, even today I use the name the priest gave me.
But I promised myself that when I had a daughter I would
call her María.— She glances up the hill to where María
is flailing over the grass.

—María, he murmurs. —Marie . . . What does your husband do?—

She feels her hands clench. —My husband is a singer.—

—Where does he perform?—

María, returning in a whirl of churning arms and swishing sundress, dives into her lap. Marta swings her from
side to side, venting the tension she feels before this gringo
whose interest she wishes neither to repel nor encourage.

María bursts into ecstatic, seesawing moans. If only Gonzalo could see her brimming face. She whispers: —He sings in the Métro.—

María wriggles free of her embrace and sits down in the grass. —My papa sings in the Métro, she recites in high, lilting French whose perfectly tuned accent astonishes Marta. —He doesn't live with us . . . *Je n'ai pas de papa, moi* . . . —

She climbs to her feet and struts away across the grass.

María! she wants to cry. But whether in reproof, dismay or guilt she can't be sure. She stares after her daughter. María has rarely strung together so many words at a stretch. The gringo looms over her, his woolly face mute. Warm summer air, softened by a tinge of humidity, courses over her shoulders. She is alone and abandoned and inadequate and now her daughter has exposed all her faults to this gruff stranger. Gonzalo, she thinks, curling into herself to escape the probing of the man's terrible, gleaming dark eyes. Her eyes are burning; her chest shakes. *Gonzalo, Gonzalo.*

The stranger leans forward, laying his broad palm on her shoulder.

EIGHTEEN ⸂

She does not look back as she leaves the park. What if the man is a spirit or a mirage? The square of paper folded into the sagging pocket of her dress might blow away in the wind. And what guarantee is paper of a man's existence? She speaks to Juan, Ana and Isabel every day, yet none of them has ever written her a letter. Though Ignacio has not written to her in months, she knows that he and Juana exist. The man in the park, who works as a researcher for a radio station and has given her his address and telephone number may disappear forever. Yet how solicitously he treated her! Even when he caressed her shoulder, his palm was soft, his hands reassuring rather than intrusive. It is not the way that men behave towards women; not the way that gringos treat Latinos. He spoke to her with a humble curiosity, as though he were backward and she modern. He regarded María as a miracle. —That man likes children, doesn't he, *hijita?*—

María replies with an admonitory, French-sounding gurgle in which Marta deciphers a complaint at leaving the park. She grips her daughter's hand as they cross the street, putting the trees and bicycle paths and fountain behind them. Stinging exhaust fumes scorch away the man's substance. She must have been dreaming. Harried by uncertainty she stops on the sidewalk, venturing a long stare in the direction of the park. Bicycle fenders glint between the trees, couples stroll beneath the glimmering shawls of green summer leaves; she cannot locate the man's large form.

—We can come back here another day. We're going to see Alfonsina now. You like that, no?—

Only Alfonsina and the Sailor will be able to tell her what this meeting means. She tingles to share her adventure with them. A gringo, a *Quebequense*, has given her his address and phone number!

She reaches into the pocket of her sundress: the folded sheet is still there. *Henri Laberge*, he has printed on the top line. Enrique, she thinks. He looks too tall and bulky and bespectacled to be an Enrique, but little matter. Pride at having sustained a conversation with him – and in French! – propels her along the sidewalk. She has not spoken to a man alone since Gonzalo left her. Was it wrong to speak to another man?

She leads Marta along Rue Rachel, the rush of cyclists on the bicycle path dividing them from the traffic. The Mountain shimmers dark green up ahead. She clutches María's hand. They are eating better now that she has paid the Ochoas the two months' back rent she owed them. Last night she cooked potatoes and rice and, to celebrate the event, a tiny rag of fatty beef (on sale for $2.06). After the meal María threw up, her stomach unable to digest so much food. From now on, Marta has promised herself, they will live as well as her government cheques allow. She does not know what will happen when her French course ends. She tries not to think about it. Perhaps Gonzalo will come back and everything will be all right; perhaps she will find a good job, paying seven or eight dollars an hour, that will enable her to support her daughter; or perhaps she and María will shrivel up and die. Her dreams bolster her faith that someone, somewhere, will step out of the welter of the city streets and look after them.

She fingers her pocket, assuring herself that the folded square of paper is still there. They walk west across Rue St-Denis and up the gentle rise to Boulevard St-Laurent.

—Alfonsina, María says. —Empanadas?—

Her pouched face blends infancy with old age, the concern in her eyes reflecting an air of venerable worry. She knows that supper is most plentiful on the days that they visit Alfonsina. They sometimes while away an entire evening talking and eating empanadas. As they prepare to leave, Marta steps in front of the cash register to pay. Alfonsina rings up the total, Marta passes her the money and Alfonsina, after laying the bills in the cash register, "makes change", handing Marta's money back to her. Alfonsina's kindness overwhelms and embarrasses and enrages her; sometimes shame keeps her away from the empanada shop for days. Then, starved of both food and companionship, she creeps back to spend three, four, five consecutive nights talking to Alfonsina.

Gripping Marta's hand, she calculates that ten or twelve days must have passed since her last visit. To put her independence to the test, she has deliberately stayed away from the empanada shop. But her encounter with the *Quebequense* has sharpened her need for counsel. They turn off St-Laurent onto Alfonsina's sidestreet. As they enter the shop, María skitters across the floor. The Sailor, holding court next to the black, formica-topped counter, hoists her up onto a barstool. The little girl's exuberance spares Marta the awkwardness of asking for food. The

Sailor and Alfonsina each receive her with a kiss as she sits down at the counter.

—*Je veux des empanadas!* María shouts.

—*Por supuesto,* if you ask me in Spanish so that I know you're a Latina.—

—*¡Por favor!* María says.

At least she makes María speak Spanish, Marta thinks. These days French seems to come most naturally to María; knowing that Marta understands French, she appears reluctant to switch. Only in church and with Alfonsina does her Spanish flow without hesitation.

—Our daughters will speak perfect French and marry *Quebequenses,* no?— Marta regrets her thoughtless words the moment she settles onto the stool next to María's. Alfonsina married late and does not have children; for a moment she looks bereft. And how can Marta raise her meeting with Enrique in a neutral tone now that she has rashly allowed the subject of marriage to *Quebequenses* to escape into the room? Forgotten aches drag at her shoulders and calves. Her first sip of Inca Kola helps revive her. She tries to devise ways of bringing up the subject of Enrique. The Sailor is regaling a troupe of *guanacos* and Guatemalans with tales of his adventures in Copenhagen during a leave from the merchant marine. She would die of shame if the men overheard her. Swallowing a second gulp of the pale-yellow soft drink, she recalls that only after moving to Montreal did she learn that Inca Kola tastes like fluoride toothpaste.

—I hope María never forgets how to speak Spanish, Alfonsina says, swabbing the counter. —If she speaks French she'll be accepted by the *Quebequenses* – —

—But she won't be accepted by the English people unless her English is also good. Why must it be like this?

My grandmother's first language was Quichua and my first language is Spanish but we are both Ecuadorean!—

—In Canada this isn't possible, Alfonsina says. —Only a few people can be Canadian; everyone else belongs to tribes.—

—This is not what I expected, Marta says. —I thought I would be accepted.—

—Ha! You thought you could marry a gringo, didn't you, my love?—

—No, I didn't. I never thought about that. I was married when I arrived here.— Spotting María's questing gaze angled in her direction, she falters. She takes a sip of Inca Kola. —I'm still married. I have a husband.—

—You haven't found a boyfriend?— Alfonsina's wry Middle Eastern face wrenches with sardonic laughter. — Someone to keep the bed warm at night and *hacer cositas?*—

—No! Marta says, her voice riding a fraction too high. The Sailor's circle falls silent. —What a waste! the Sailor says, laughing from his belly. He slaps a paunchy man across the shoulders. —How about you, Pepe? You're hard up, why don't you give her a try?— The men snicker. Pepe sneaks a glance at Marta. —Keep your eyes to yourself, degenerate! Alfonsina says.

The men laugh again, but this time their laughter is directed at Pepe.

—¡*Pobrecita*!— Alfonsina's voice dips into a studied off-hand tone Marta interprets as an apology for her husband. —So young and pretty, too!— Alfonsina's parents were devout Syrian immigrants but she is a ribald Colombian *costeña* to her core. *Una mujer burda*, Marta thinks. Her Andean reserve is sometimes offended by Alfonsina's uncouth Caribbean exuberance. If Alfonsina has grown up so profoundly Colombian, isn't there hope that María may grow up Québécoise? Perhaps she will be the one to marry a gringo.

Marta drains her Inca Kola, cherishing Enrique's image in silence. She tries to think of a reply to the chorus of laughter, but no reply is possible. Everything has been spoiled; she cannot raise the subject of Enrique. Once she has served them, Alfonsina snaps a *cumbia* cassette into the tapedeck and clops along behind the counter on her heels, striking the black formica in time with the jouncing beat. Marta fidgets on her stool. If I'm uncomfortable here, she thinks, how will I feel out on the street?

Nineteen ꝑ

In August, when her French course ends, cutting off the flow of her cheques, she finds a job in a warehouse behind a clothing factory. She packs dresses into boxes. Her shift runs from seven to three-thirty with half an hour for lunch. The four dollars fifty cents an hour she is paid barely compensates for the loss of her COFI money and the replacement of COFI's daycare centre with a measly child-care subsidy. She is financially worse off than she was before she started working. Each week she falls farther behind; one of these months she will be unable to scrape together the rent money.

She works with Haitian and Turkish and Guatemalan women, a few impoverished Portuguese and Vietnamese, and others whose countries of origin remain obscure. During her months at COFI she met people from all over the world. She knows the names and problems of a dozen countries she hadn't heard of before signing up to learn French. But all this information is useless to her at work. Her hopes of continuing to learn and discover and improve her French are stifled by a rule that forbids speaking on the warehouse floor. On the bus home the women tease each other in a mixture of English, French and clashing accents of Spanish about small incidents that have occurred during the day. At lunch the other women gab over their sandwiches as they sit on the barren cloak-room floor. Marta, who can rarely afford to bring food, prefers to curl up on the concrete, leaning into a corner if one is available, and fall asleep. Her eyes have only to slip shut for her grandmother's voice to swoop down. *Pwwaway, Martita! Nuqanchis cieloman risanchis.* Fly, little Marta! We are going to Heaven . . . In her midday reveries Heaven becomes a desolate canyon floor crossed by a boiling brown river where she hauls buckets of water back to the house in the company of Juan, Ana and Isabel. Heaven is a village where everyone knows her and every-one speaks Spanish, even though her grandmother prefers Quichua. Brown people sneer at black people, and white people from Quito are better than either, but being poor doesn't matter as much because everyone is poor. When she wakes nothing makes sense. Her only possible salva-tion, now that the forgiving face of Jesus Christ has re-ceded, lies in binding herself to a reliable man who will support and protect her. But she does not know if she can trust men. Yet in the absence of a village and a river and a family, does she have a choice?

But how many men have shown an interest in her? How many have been enchanted by María? At work she meets only other women. When she closes her eyes, Enrique's soft, bearded face smiles at her through the summer heat. Two weeks after meeting him, she took María back to Parc Lafontaine, turned her loose and scanned the grass for Enrique. Darting across the slope dropping to the edge of the upper pond, María attracted the attention of squir-rels, pigeons, stray dogs and other small children. But the large man whose glasses and receding hairline she found so reassuring remained invisible.

The other women shake her awake at the end of the lunch break. The afternoons stream past on the patchwork of her midday visions. She pirouettes around the cemetery with Juan, Ana and Isabel, she peels potatoes and creeps into Ignacio's shop to watch the men settle their unhurried transactions for wax and soap and fruit. Behind it all, magnified by the heat of the clamorous warehouse, throb thoughts of Enrique, Enrique, Enrique . . . He is her secret, her strength: the glow that warms her strained, hard-working loneliness. He is her hope of assuaging the city rhythms that batter her. He is the promise that her life will not always be an ordeal.

Riding the bus home at three-thirty, she feels too distracted to join in the end-of-the-day banter. The other women are all going home to husbands. She is plagued by a foggy vision, wavering before her mind's eye, of a phantom white-skinned protector. She must talk to someone about Enrique; if she tries to hold him inside her any longer, she will burst.

Strands of fabric abrade the flesh beneath her fingernails; the smell of cardboard impregnates her nostrils. Her day at work has given her a headache, but it doesn't matter. She picks up María at the daycare centre and heads for the main entrance of the Jean-Talon Métro station. She will find Alfonsina and tell her everything. It doesn't matter how Alfonsina reacts, it doesn't matter if the Sailor and his drunken friends are there; even a disparaging response will relieve the pressure. She remembers with discomfort her stuttering attempts to discuss her internal torments with the missionaries at the Evangelical Church of God. Despite all they have done to save her from despair, the polite young men from Alberta and Alabama cannot provide her with the consolation of a scourging Catholic confession.

—Come on, she says, prodding María onto the escalator. The trip four stops down to the Plateau Mont-Royal will cost her nothing: she has bought a monthly pass to get to work, and María is still short enough to slip under the bar without paying.

The stale lukewarm air rising from the underground platforms sunken deep in the earth flows thick with reverberating chords of music. María bobs up and down on the escalator step. Her hands glide to the music's lazy, pipe-pierced beat. Her eyes look dreamy and distant.

—Come on, Marta says, taking her hand. The music aggravates her headache. She hustles her daughter along the broad passage, wondering how best to introduce the subject of Enrique to Alfonsina. Why can't she forget about him?

In the dim light of the crowded mezzanine she spots the source of the music. She stops, squeezing her daughter's hand.

—*Maman!?* María says, as though Marta has pinched her.

The musicians, their eyes fixed on the stems of their instruments, sway before her like men in a trance. Do they belong to the village or to the city whose pulsations are bearing her across the mezzanine floor? They wear waist-length ponchos, woollen Andean earflap hats. One man puffs on a *rondador*, another tweaks at a *charango*. An inverted felt hat sits before them on a wad of folded, embroidered cloth. A brittle clinking sound cuts through the clacking of heels and the grumble and yell of conversation stirred up by the rush-hour throngs. A coin falls into the hat. Following its trajectory, she makes out a white-capped bottle of Naya mineral water standing on the floor in the lee of the musicians' piled instrument cases. The guitar case, scuffed along the edges around its wrinkled MIAMI decal, belongs to Gonzalo.

She stares at the guitarist. He is a small man, his form shrunken beneath the wide wings of his poncho. His heavy mustache clings to his face like a glossy leech, sapping his cheeks of vigour. His hair falls past his shoulders.

A train whooshes in along the southbound platform at the bottom of the staircase.

—*Maman!* María says. —*On va manquer le métro!*—

He will never come back to her. Why hasn't she understood this until now? Stunned by the city, he has relapsed into a past he has never lived. A past Marta never intends to live. I *will* be modern, I *will* give María a future, I *will* marry a strong man who is not afraid to belong here.

Anger and habit propel her forward a step. But there is no longer any reason for her to greet or berate him. They are strangers; it will confuse María to be told that this man is her father.

The high-tech hum of the southbound train pulling out of the station makes her pause. Gonzalo's head rolls up, his eyes bathing her with the hangdog supplication of a practised appeal for funds. He reels off a rippling, flirtatious chord that jars through his neighbours' monotonous piping and twanging. Beneath the swaddling of his mustache, thick hair and backward costume, a young soldier's smooth face gazes at her in dawning, perplexed recognition.

She turns away, bundling María onto the up-escalator. María cries out. —*¡Apúrate!* Marta says. —Move it!—

They lope up the moving stairs until they are both gasping for breath.

—*¡Marta!¡Marta! ¡Mi amorcita!*—

His voice hollers after her one more time before fading into a forlorn, inebriated dirge.

María has burst into tears. —Alfonsina!— In Spanish, she says: —I want to see Alfonsina!—

—Not today. We'll visit Alfonsina soon, but this evening I'm busy.— She catches her breath and leans forward over her daughter's shoulder. —Your mami has been very stupid. She forgot that there was someone else it is more important for her to visit than Alfonsina.—

TWENTY ❧

Three months, she thinks. Three months without communicating with him because I still considered myself Gonzalo's wife. Three months' silence because I refused to accept that my husband was no longer my husband. Enrique. She savours the syllables. Enrique, whose real name is Henri, who is a man breathing the air of this city, not a vision from my village, who may have found another woman by now – if he didn't have one before. The boundary dividing living and dead, being and phantom – so fluid in the village, so unforgiving in the city – has tripped her up again. That, and her stupid leftover loyalty to Gonzalo.

She must go to see him. He gave her his address and telephone number; she, in her bewilderment, failed to give him hers. The telephone confuses her. Only the sight of his face can assuage her confusion.

Impatience nags at her as she bathes and feeds María and sits her down in front of the television where the *guanaco* children are taking desultory stabs at their homework between comments on the actors whose faces fill the screen. At María's first nod of drowsiness, Marta whisks her into the back room. After putting her to bed, she slips across the room and unfolds the map of the city Gonzalo bought during his stint as a salesman. She locates Enrique's apartment near the Mont-Royal Métro station.

Ignoring *Señora* Ochoa's stare, she pulls on her coat and heads towards the door.

—Don't come back late, *Señora* Ochoa says, or you'll wake my husband.— The children's heads turn, sad *guanaco* reproach filming their eyes.

—I have to get up early for work, too, Marta says, closing the door behind her.

What a relief to escape the apartment! She lives for the day when she will share an apartment only with her daughter and husband. My new husband. She tries to get used to the idea. Gonzalo is gone, disappeared, no longer part of my life. He will never again act like a responsible husband. I must find someone else.

Her resolution encloses her spine in an uneasy grip; her cheeks and forehead flood with heat. What will they say if she has two husbands? Even lascivious Juana might not let her in the door. But she cannot continue to live as she is living now; she must give María a father as Juana gave her one. She never thought she would see Juana as having succeeded where she had failed.

She skirts the Métro station, afraid that Gonzalo's group may still be playing there, and walks out to Rue St-Denis to catch a southbound 30 bus. During the long wait at the bus stop she draws slow, steadying breaths, imposing calm on her traitorous body. She wipes at her eyes and combs her hair. This is no way to present herself to Enrique.

She gets off the bus at the intersection of Avenue du Mont-Royal and walks eastward through the chilly autumn darkness into streets of run-together walk-ups. Enrique's building, a modern apartment block, is set among a row of spiral-staircased brick and stone triplexes. A young man precedes her into the building, opens the main door with a key and holds it for her, sparing her the complication of buzzing.

—*Merci, monsieur,* she murmurs, following him inside.

Three months, she thinks, picking her way up the stairs. What if he's eating supper with his wife and children?

When she reaches the third floor the door of his apartment, clearly numbered, brings her to a halt. She stares and stares at the varnished wood. She cannot do this. It is not a thing for a woman to do.

Footsteps and voices approach along the corridor. Two women round the corner, come to a stop and deal her long, inquiring looks.

She raises her hand and knocks.

When the door opens, she concentrates on the big blunt head stooping towards her, the face flustered behind the steel-rimmed glasses. Was this really him, his face wan in the pallid light? She struggles to imagine these slack, pasty cheeks baked by the humid glare of a summer afternoon in Parc Lafontaine. —I'm not interested, he says, and begins to swing the door shut.

—Don't you remember me?—

The door stops. He looks at her. —Where's your daughter?—

—The family I live with is looking after María.— She catches her hands smoothing her dress. Can he tell that a few minutes earlier she was nearly sobbing?

A hissing noise makes him turn his head. When he looks back at her, he edges his body sideways. —Come in.—

She steps in the door. Bookshelves and French-language posters and a luxurious-looking couch; the television not perched on the kitchen counter but presiding sedately over a living-room coffee table all its own; stacked cassettes

of *música norteamericana* in French; a flat black box wired
to the telephone; a glimpse of a huge, solid bed with four
carved bedposts as he leads her down the hall, slippers of
clown-like fluffiness enlarging his feet: this is the first time
she has set foot in one of *their* apartments.

He leads her onto the balcony overlooking the street.
He thumps the wooden sign he has strapped to the railing,
facing out over the sidewalk: *NE TOUCHEZ PAS A LA LOI 101.*
When she leans over the railing to read it, he explains that
it is a response to the threat to his language. His words
warm her. How kind he is to react so well to her intrusion,
relieving her of the burden of making conversation.

She looks out at the steep-gabled, wooden-staircased
stone triplexes butting against the darkness. —You've got
a beautiful view. Our room doesn't have windows.—

He looks uncertain. —Would you like a cup of coffee?—

—Thank you.— She follows him back into the living
room.

He comes to a halt, his hands hanging at his sides. —I'm
cooking supper. If you're going to stay for coffee, you
might as well eat supper.—

She looks down at the polished hardwood, suddenly
uncomfortable. —You are very kind.—

He veers his big body close to hers. —Now that you're
staying for supper, he says, his voice swinging into a cava-
lier lilt, you can help me *éplucher les patates.*—

His kitchen is a separate room, not a place sharing the
functions of eating and television watching. Each cupboard door he opens reveals gleaming ranks of plates, a
wondrous variety of pots and pans stacked inside and on
top of each other. He has a microwave oven and a glass
coffee pot. Ah, she thinks, at last I'm in Canada!

He gestures in the direction of the potatoes arrayed on an oval-shaped wooden board on the counter. —Could you *éplucher* them, please? I'll season the steak and chop up the tomatoes.—

She presses her lips shut, her cheeks flooding with agitated heat. The sight of a man cooking stymies her. She has heard that gringo men cook, yet this burly man's unashamed fussing over womanly chores brings her to a halt. Can she still respect him as a man? How can she be sure that he is not a *maricón*? And what does *éplucher* mean? What is he expecting her to do with the potatoes? The thought that she may disappoint him terrifies her.

He frowns at her. Then, his expression clearing, he grasps a utensil she has not noticed lying amid the shiny clutter of the counter. He brushes it over the skin of the nearest potato, shearing away shavings to reveal the white meat beneath.

Pelar, she thinks. *Éplucher* means *pelar*. —*Éplucher!* she says with a small shout of exultation. She repeats the word.

His startled expression eases into a slow smile.

—In my country, she says, trying to offer him wisdom of her own in exchange for the word he has added to her vocabulary, we eat potatoes every day. But we don't peel them; we can't afford to waste the goodness in the skin.—

—In Quebec, he says, potatoes are not an important part of our culture, but peeling is.— In the autumn families come together for the *épluchette de blé d'Inde*, the final outdoor gathering before the onset of winter. In his family it is his aunt and uncle who host the *épluchette de blé d'Inde;* every year he drives out to the suburbs to roast Indian corn in their backyard.

She feels confused. *Pelar* the corn? With a peeler? She continues flicking at the potato's skin with the utensil he has handed her. Thin brown strips spray onto the counter. —It must take a very long time to get the corn ready to eat. Only a people who do not suffer hunger could take so much time to peel corn.—

His laughter makes her ache with discomfort. —Not *éplucher* like this, he says, snapping his wrist as though whittling down a corn cob. —*Éplucher* like this.— She leaps back as he swipes his hand before her face, imitating the motions of a peasant husking a corn cob.

—But that is not peeling, she complains. When she husks a corn cob she does not say *pelar* but *descascarar*. If *pelar* is *éplucher*, then shouldn't *descascarar* be matched to a different French verb? Yet they are the same. It exasperates her. These French people demand such precision of foreigners who speak their language, yet they –

—Of course that's peeling, he says.

—No, it isn't.—

He smiles, meeting her eyes. They begin lunging around the small kitchen, each acting out a private reverie of picking and peeling. His cumbersome, weighed-down jig makes her reel with laughter. The silky greying hair on his high forehead lifts as he bobs up and down with Latin brio; he might be chanting a *cumbia*. Her own movements feel lithe and delicate. Delighted by this escape from her worries, this sudden plunge into abandonment, she gyrates her hips and whoops with laughter.

He reaches out to hold her.

She jumps back, banging her shoulder blades into the ridged panel of the refrigerator door. A loose strand of hair falls over her forehead.

—I'm sorry, Marta.— He drags a long breath up through his barrel chest. —Let's finish making supper.—

Idiot! Fool! How could she be so stupid? How will she make it up to him? What if she has lost him for good? What if he never again tries to touch her? She longs to construct a gesture that will overleap all ambiguity, making clear her eagerness to belong to him.

She watches his soft, square-fingered hands seasoning the steak and slicing the tomatoes. All the men she has known before have had calluses and broken fingernails. The pliant white gloves of Enrique's hands give her nothing to fear, yet they also make her less sure about what to expect of him. Returning to his side at the counter, she slices and rinses the potatoes. They sizzle as they strike the frying pan. He keeps his head bowed as he disappears into the dining room to lay the table. What does he think of her? Men in this country, she knows, expect women to fall into bed with them at the merest hint of interest. He must regard her as cruel and cold and foreign. How can she draw herself closer to him? Can she bring herself to do what he so clearly expects of her?

As they eat supper, he appears to forget their misunderstanding. He describes the *épluchettes de blé d'Inde* that his aunt and uncle hold in the backyard: there is music, hordes of nephews and nieces and neighbours and cousins, abundant corn and many other types of food. —If you want to know the best and worst of Quebec, he says, you have only to watch my family eating corn.—

Beneath the table, her ankles tremble. She cannot insult him by refusing a second invitation. Struggling to overcome the slippery uncertainty of speaking French and her dread fear of doing wrong – she is still Gonzalo's wife! – she says: —Thank you very much. I'll be happy to come. It's very kind of you to invite me.—

Absorbed in masticating a slice of meat, he does not reply. His eyes glisten behind his glasses. Didn't he want her to say yes? How strange these gringos are, never expressing the slightest sign of joy or gratitude. According to her COFI teachers, the Québécois are Latin like her. If Enrique is Latin, why is he chewing in indomitable silence?

He points to her plate. —Aren't you hungry?—

She has left most of her food untouched.

—I want to take it home to heat up for María. And for my brother Juan and my sisters Ana and Isabel.— Why must her brother and sisters intrude? She does not wish them to know about Enrique. Not now; not yet. What if they spread word through the village that she is having dinner with a man who is not her husband? How will she be received when she returns?

—I didn't realize you had so many mouths to feed, Enrique says. —Please take more. Don't limit yourself to leftovers.—

He stacks her half-full plate on top of his empty one and carries them into the kitchen. She follows him out of the dining room, her eyes tracing the varied softnesses of his fluffy slippers, thick woollen sweater and tangled woolly beard. His large hands wrap her steak and tomatoes in separate sheets of tinfoil. He opens the refrigerator door and begins piling food onto the counter. He pulls a plastic container from a cupboard above his head and packs a slab of cheese, an apple and two cookies on top of the steak and tomatoes. —For your daughter.—

She accepts the plastic container with her left hand, floundering to find a way to express her gratitude, her yearning to make him hers. Does he understand? She knows that, as with Gonzalo, there is only one way to convey this message.

She catches his wrist. A hard flare of bone, flanked by tightly strung veins, resists her fingertips. The warmth of his skin fills her with a determined, desperate self-confidence. She tugs and tugs on his arm until he jerks forward. Yoked together, they stumble across the hall dividing the kitchen from the bedroom.

He meets her eyes through the lenses of his glasses. Glancing towards the bed, he shakes his hand until she releases him. —Marta . . . —

—I must thank you.—

Understanding focusses his eyes with a bright gleam. —No.—

She grips his hand again. —Please. I don't want to owe you anything.—

—You owe me nothing.—

Her throat shudders. —Men always think I'm ugly . . . —

—That's not the question.— His sharp tone makes her burst into tears. —You're not ugly, he says in a rush. —But we don't know each other.—

He reaches for her.

She writhes away from him, tightening her grip on the plastic container. She stumbles down the hall to the door of the apartment.

The doorhandle turns but the door does not open. She wrestles with the metal knob for a moment, then realizes that she has forgotten to snap back the bolt.

—Wait, Enrique says.

She steps into the hall. When did she start crying like this?

—Marta!— His level shoulders fill the doorway. —Please say you'll come to my family's corn roast.—

※

—Come to bed, Marta, he says, laying his palm on her shoulder.

—Where is she?— She cups her hands around her face, pressing them against the cool window pane. Leaves from the neighbour's maples, soaked by yesterday's rain and drained of their bright colours by the darkness, lie plastered against the hump of the lawn. The street is silent. —It's nearly three in the morning. Oh God, something's happened. She's had an accident . . . —

His grip on her shoulder tightens. —You can't worry about her forever. She has to grow up.—

—Not yet. *She's barely sixteen!*— She straightens up, pulling away from the curtains. —I *tried* to give her a decent upbringing . . . —

—Marta . . . —

His hug irritates her even as it relieves the pressure contracting her throat. He's going to feel so good about himself, she thinks, going limp against his chest. He's going to go upstairs and fall asleep in the comfort of having fulfilled his husbandly duty.

But she won't relax for a second until María comes home. If her daughter's life goes wrong, the blame reverts to her. She can hardly meet his eyes. Swallowing against the tightness in her throat, she says: —I can't stop wondering when . . . where . . . I could have done something different.—

TWENTY ONE ℘

I'll come, she says.

One foot in his apartment, the other in the hall, she hugs his plastic container against her stomach. The tussle of wills is beginning: he does not want her to leave. His big shambling form will enfold her. Might she win back Gonzalo through his astonished jealousy at her having snared a *Quebequense*? She is someone special: her destiny refuses to be thwarted. Gonzalo can abandon her, starve her, ruin María's childhood, but all his destructive spite cannot prevent her from attracting a better man to invite her to meet his family.

She smooths her dress as Enrique blunders towards her. His big arms flop around her shoulders; the scorched lysol smell of his heavily-soaped flesh enshrouds her. He will rend her body with his hard whiteness, purging her of the backward stain of a dark woman who has presented her husband with an even darker daughter. Gonzalo, draped in a poncho he would have disdained at home, has cloaked himself in lies about the past; she will dazzle him with the truth of a gringo marriage. She imagines his mustache sagging in dismay when he learns that she has settled into Enrique's apartment. Then, at last, she will be able to forget him.

But to reach that moment she must give herself over to Enrique's large, padded hands. She must become whoever he wishes her to become, embodying his every illusion as she did for Gonzalo.

He kisses her cheek. She waits for his mouth to seek out hers. The demons in her have subsided. A few minutes ago she would have yowled like Juana in the cold canyon night if his hands had grazed her thigh. But now despair, complicated by his sudden reversal of mood, plagues her with nervous uncertainty. In providing her with food, wasn't he proposing that they assume the roles of man and wife? Having choked off her rising excitement, he begins to fondle her. Why didn't he take her when she offered him the chance? Couldn't he behave like an *hombre*?

—I hardly know you, he says, his hands dropping to his sides. —But I want to know you better.—

Voices waft along the corridor, accompanied by the thud of boots. Laying his hand on her forearm, Enrique guides her back into the apartment. He closes the door. His gentleness comforts her; he does not grab or push or order her around. She reminds herself that Gonzalo, too, appeared gentle until he got a guitar in his hands and began to bask in the villagers' stupid adulation, until they married and were living together, until he had a daughter to support.

She lifts her eyes to read the expression in Enrique's bespectacled face, her back flush against the wall. It is coming now, it must be coming. He kisses her on the side of the mouth. Their mouths open and for a moment her tongue is yielding and seeking with a thirst that pulls aching memories from the pit of her stomach to her staggering brain. But as she reaches up for a firmer purchase, they slip apart. He withdraws to his stout height, peering at her from beneath pursed grey eyebrows. Worried about what he may think of her, she says: —Do you know me better now?—

—I was married for ten years.—

Thank God! Thank God it is nothing more than that. And he said *was.* —I was married for four years.— Her voice wrenches into an abashed squeak. This common ground frightens her. It does not feel right to speak of her marriage as over; legally, in the eyes of God, the marriage endures. She cannot bear for Gonzalo never, ever to return to her. She will shrivel with mortification if people begin to think of her as a *divorciada.* Even shameless Juana has always stuck by Ignacio. —My mother is a witch. She cast a spell on my father to make him marry her.—

His face goes blank. His eyes narrow behind his glasses. —And in Quebec you live with your sisters and your brother?—

—No, I live with *guanacos.* My brother and sisters are not here. But they are always with me.—

A frown passes across his face. He gestures towards the plastic container. —And the food?—

—The food is for María.—

—I'd like to see Marie again, he says. —My wife and I didn't have children.— The heavy, crusted-looking lines of his face soften. His frowning perplexity vanishes. —Will you bring her to my aunt's corn roast?—

He offers to pick her up in his car.

—No.— She shakes her head. One glimpse of a gringo in a car, and the Ochoas will raise her rent. —I'll meet you in front of the Jean-Talon Métro station.—

She lingers, curling her fingers around the knob of the doorhandle, to allow him time to detain her. When he reaches over her shoulder, though, it is only to hold the door for her. She feels wounded. Perhaps his reticence shows respect, but a nervous ache in her chest tells her that her meagre body has proved too skimpy and dark-skinned for his taste. Either he is a cowardly man who admires her or a worthwhile man who is rejecting her. Scurrying along the shadowed sidewalk towards the Mont-Royal Métro station, she jams the plastic container against her stomach to stave off the despair pressing down on her lungs in the November chill.

TWENTY TWO ♪

M aría is asleep when she slips into the room. Marta rolls onto the pad alongside her, closing her arms around her daughter's softly breathing body. María feels tiny and delicate; Marta would die to give her food. She kisses her dark forehead just below the hairline. To-morrow she will heat up the meat and tomatoes into a surprise hot breakfast.

In the dark, a thrilling excitement supplants her doubts about Enrique. He remembered her! She has become friends with a prosperous *Quebequense*. The bond is a treas-ure; it makes her feel as good as other Latinos. Last week-end, passing the open door of a boutique on Rue St-Denis, she bowed her head on hearing two elegant Venezuelan women with glistening stockings and gold flashing from their ears quizzing a shop clerk in English. She feels stifled by the hordes of *guanacos* diligently organizing their per-petual round of dances and parties; she envies them their incestuously close community and their weekly phone calls home to San Salvador, San Miguel or San Vicente. (The village doesn't have phone service. Even if it did, how could she afford a phone call to Ecuador?) The Mexicans, most of whom, according to Alfonsina, have arrived only recently, have already become prosperous enough to set up their own shops and drive big cars. The Chileans, erudite and established, speaking both French and English, intimidate her despite their comical accents.

The alarm clock that she bought for ten dollars at the Jean Coutu pharmacy launches its insistent squeak at a quarter to five. Gloom crashes over her, reviving the desperation that panicked her into visiting Enrique. It is only the second time in her life that she has summoned herself to act with such brazen forwardness; unlike her decision to dance with Gonzalo in the barracks, last night's visit failed to change her life. The weight of Enrique's rejection bears down behind her gritty eyes. She wakes María, dresses her and leads her to the bathroom. The four *guanaco* children sleeping on the living room floor have not stirred, but *Señor* Ochoa has beaten her to the toilet. She sits down in the kitchen, rocking María on her lap. The girl mumbles to her in French spiked with Spanish and English. Marta replies in firm Spanish. *Señor* Ochoa, sleepy eyed but immaculately shaven, bumbles out of the bathroom. His sock-encased feet swish across the linoleum. They exchange muted formalities.

When she and Marta emerge from the bathroom, the refrigerator door stands open. *Señora* Ochoa has peeled back the lid of Enrique's plastic container and is sniffing the contents. Marta plunges forward and grabs the container. —That's mine! A friend gave it to me.—

—Oh, so she has *amiguitos* now. That didn't take long, did it? I warn you, if you even try to tempt my husband I'll tear your eyes out. Don't think that I don't hear the two of you whispering every morning. Just because you couldn't hold onto your husband . . . —

—Your husband doesn't interest me. My *Quebequense* friend . . . —

—A gringo!— *Señora* Ochoa cuffs at her disarrayed hair. Lack of sleep has sapped her brown skin of its lustre. —Now you can afford to pay me a fair rent.—

—I already pay you too much. And he's not giving me money.—

—Ha! She's doing it for nothing!—

—Be quiet! Marta says, startled by her own ferocity. —He knows I'm a *señora decente*. He treats me with respect.—

Before *Señora* Ochoa can reply, Cayetano and Roque bounce into the kitchen. Don't children feel tired in the morning? Marta turns away, reaching for the long-handled frying pan on the counter.

—You see, *Señora* Ochoa says, we take the *negrita* in off the street and she uses our frying pan without permission and doesn't so much as offer to share her food with us.—

Marta makes breakfast in sweltering silence. She refuses to look at the Ochoas while she scrubs the frying pan. María toys with her food. She smears the tomatoes across the plate with her fork and probes the meat, which Marta has diced into small squares, with her fingers. When she has finished scrubbing the pan, Marta sits down at the table and forces María to eat.

Her daughter's dark eyes give a teasing flicker as she twists her head around to avoid the food Marta is thrusting towards her mouth. She tries to draw out breakfast in an effort to delay Marta's departure. Normally they have so little to eat that Marta welcomes the tactic: it fosters the illusion that breakfast has been a full meal. Now she panics. Any leftover food she returns to the refrigerator will have been fed to the *guanaco* children by the time she arrives at work. María refuses a slice of tomato, then sticks out her tongue at the diced meat.

—Are you sure you don't want it? Marta asks.

María shakes her head. —I'm full.—

Late for work, Marta gobbles down the remaining morsels and runs for the bus.

Twenty Three ♪

The night before Enrique's corn roast, Alfonsina phones her.

— The Sailor ran into Gonzalo, she says.

—In the Métro? Marta asks, pressing her hand over her free ear to mute the blare of the television.

—No. In Parc Jeanne-Mance.— Gonzalo and Rodrigo were reclining on a park bench below the soccer fields drinking beer from bottles sheathed in brown paper bags. Each time a generously endowed young Latina ambled past, they would try to lure her over: —*Ay, Mamita! Ven acá, mi amor. No te enojes, Mamita.*—

Alfonsina's imitation makes Marta wince. She huddles against the kitchen counter. *Señora* Ochoa brushes past her. —Please, Alfonsina. I can't stand it. *No aguanto.*—

—No, but listen, there's more. The Sailor went over to talk to him— —

—I don't want to hear it. He was playing in the Jean-Talon Métro and he saw me and started shouting. I'm not going back to him, Alfonsina.—

—He's doing well, Marta. The Sailor couldn't believe it when Gonzalo told him, but he's asked around and it's true. Gonzalo's going to be playing guitar on an album by a *Quebequense* singer, one of the ones you hear on French radio. And his own group will be in a café the weekend after next.—

My husband's name on a gringo cassette. No one in the village will believe it. They'll worship him when we go back. —Which café? she asks. One of the *guanaco* children vents a stagey sigh, walks across the room and turns up the volume on the television.

—On Rue St-Denis, just north of Mont-Royal. I think you should go and see him.—

Will he wear his clown suit, she wonders, and his stupid poncho? Doesn't he remember how smart he used to look in his uniform and his suit? She hopes he will dress in a way that will make the gringos respect him. Yet if he's become successful, why does he cry out at women from park benches? It is obvious that he needs a wife. Thank God he hasn't fallen captive to some empty-headed young girl. He is missing the discipline imposed by having a family.

—Will you go? Alfonsina asks. —I'll go with you if you want.—

—No, that's not necessary . . . — She draws her breath high and tight in her chest. —I met a *Quebequense*. He invited me to his family's corn roast tomorrow night.—

Señora Ochoa, shuttling sideways along the kitchen counter, thumps her hip into Marta's side. The *guanaco* children are staring at her over their closed schoolbooks. The girl, Ana María, thrusts her head forward, straining to distinguish her every murmur through the hysterical clamour of a television show about a family of black people living in a mansion-like house. —What does he do? Alfonsina asks.

—He's a researcher for Radio Québec, she whispers, as *Señora* Ochoa jostles her again. —Oh, it doesn't feel right, Alfonsina, he's not my husband . . . —

Cayetano and Roque snicker.

—Shut up! Marta says, turning on them. Returning to the receiver, she says: —It's a week after the corn roast. If things go well with Enrique . . . — Astonished at her own bloodless calculations, she falls silent. —I don't know who I'll be in a week's time, Alfonsina.—

—Wait and see, Alfonsina says. —I think you should be there to applaud Gonzalo, Marta. This corn roast – —

—Oh, I want to go to them both! Is there anything wrong with that?— She stares at the wall, trying to take refuge deep in her mind. Her grandmother's Quichua whispers rustle through the hectic air of the apartment: *Tutahucha, Martita. Tutahucha.* But as yet, she has committed no night-sin. —I'll try to go to both, Alfonsina. No matter who I am then.—

—You'll always be a Latina, Marta.—

—I'm living here now. It's only natural for me to have *Quebequense* friends.—

—Your name is still Marta, it's not Marthe.—

—I want to see him again – —

—Who? Alfonsina asks.

—My husband – — She stops in confusion, brought to a halt by Alfonsina's censure. Alfonsina has told Marta that she had many lovers before marrying the Sailor, yet serious gaps exist in her understanding. Marriage solved many of Alfonsina's problems. Can't she see that marriage itself can become a horrendous problem? Alfonsina has never feared for her next meal or worried about a child. —I'll come and see you soon, Alfonsina. We'll talk then, no?—

—*Claro*. We'll talk. *Chau*.—

She hangs up and heads towards the back room, ignoring the *guanacos*' silence.

—*Oh, Alfonsina, he's not my husband,* Cayetano mimics.

Marta slams the door behind her and sits down on the foam pad, tugging María against her side.

She and Enrique speak little the next evening during the drive to the suburbs. Her grandmother's crooked shadow darkens the back seat of Enrique's car. The frail wittering of Father Alberto's sermons, sown into the static of the car radio, undermines each upbeat tune that comes bouncing off the dashboard. She longs to ask the man beside her to turn the car around.

If she falls in love with him, he may not permit her to be present when Gonzalo takes the stage.

—Where's Marie? he said when he picked her up.

—She's at home. It's her bedtime.—

—Who's looking after her?—

—The family I'm living with, but I don't trust them.—

—Why not?— He squinted through his glasses into the patterns of light streaming ahead of them through the darkness.

—They're Salvadorean.—

It was clear that he didn't understand.

After long minutes of silence he turns off the autoroute onto a road running between suburban houses like the ones she has seen on television. Breaking the silence, he asks: —Do you want to have more children?—

She does not know what to say.

They drive to a suburb bordered by fields. He pulls up in front of a house darkened by the white lights glaring in its backyard. Climbing out of the car, she hears slow, emotional *música norteamericana.*

—What beautiful music.—

Enrique grunts and leads her around the side of the house. The wide backyard, fringed with deck chairs, is crowded with people of all ages. Tables lined with sandwiches and soft drinks surround the grill where teenagers are roasting corn cobs. A wooden platform projecting from the back of the house dominates the yard like a control post. She staggers against the blur of voices and faces. Enrique's hand closes around hers. He leads her up the steps onto the platform and introduces her to his parents, a distant elderly couple bundled into twin deck chairs. They regard her with hard, confused expressions. She paws the varnished boards of the platform with her sneakers. Everyone else is *Quebequense*. The brown and black faces visible on downtown streets alarmed her during her first weeks in Montreal, but in this laundered suburb she feels bereft.

—We don't have to stay long if you're worried about your daughter, Enrique whispers.

—It's charming, she says.

He leads her down the wooden steps onto the grass, introducing her to family and friends: strange faces and curious names too numerous to remember. A fresh gale of music soars from the speakers and everyone under sixty hops down onto the damp grass to dance in a huge, swaying circle.

—The Québécois are real Latins, she says.

Enrique smiles, but does not suggest that they join the crowd, who have linked hands and are swinging each other around, feet skidding on the dewy grass. I wish María could be here instead of me, she thinks: I wish I could make her part of this world without having to endure it myself.

The music stops. Up on the platform, a pudgy teenage boy grips a microphone and croons in a voice far more seductive than his appearance. Enrique grumbles and kicks at the grass.

—What a pretty song, she says.

—He's singing in English. He doesn't even understand what he's saying. What alienation!—

—Singers are egotists. They only think about themselves.—

Her shoulders tremble. He swallows her in his long arms, hauling her against his body. Remembering the taste of his mouth, she waits for the demons to rise in her. They hobble around the grass, squashed together too tightly to dance.

He stumbles to a halt, his big right hand stiffening against her hip.

—What's the matter?—

—My brother-in-law, he says. —He's never had a decent job, so he gets drunk and my sister has to discipline him like a child.—

On the opposite side of the yard a determined-looking woman and her thickset husband are wrestling. The woman shakes the man by his twisted lapels. Four children watch the couple with rapt concentration. The woman seizes the man's wrist, hauling him out of the yard and onto the street.

I should have fought harder to hold onto him, Marta thinks. But by the time she realized he was straying, it was too late. She watches the children drawing back. They observe their parents with a subdued, hurt knowingness that she surprises on occasion in María's eyes. Yet as they scatter over the grass amid friends and cousins, Enrique's despair confounds her. —Your sister is a strong woman and a good mother.—

—But our men are so pathetic!—

—It is a woman's job to keep her family together.—

He drags her against his big body with unnerving force. What's wrong with him? How can he feel ill at ease among so many dancing relatives?

Música norteamericana, she thinks, writhing to the slumberous beat in an effort to twist free of Enrique's hug. Barefoot on the cold concrete floor, stripping off her clothes for him; watching his eyes, knowing he is her only chance of escaping the village.

—Marta!—

—What? she asks, her feet swishing through the damp grass. The pungent smack of corn roasted on street-corner stalls prickling her nostrils the day of her arrival in Quito; the sight of city dwellers munching on corn startling her. In the village they ate potatoes; corn was cultivated by Indians up on the *páramo.*

—Put your shoes on! Everyone's looking.—

—*Los campesinos suelen andar descalzos y yo soy campesina, mi amor.*— Gonzalo's father treating her with disdain because she comes from the country; her dark skin and thick features betraying her mother's blackness. Gonzalo's own mother, safely dead, veiled in a worshipful halo of adulation: her mannerisms, her rules, her origins – everything about her deemed beyond reproach or inquiry. His sisters referring to Marta as Gonzalo's peasant girl. *La campesina.* Saying it in her hearing.

—Speak French, he says. —I can't understand you.—

The music sighs to a crescendo. Batteries are not sapped of their potency in this country, electricity never seems to be in short supply; everything functions flawlessly except

for the people. The fat boy on the platform blushes at the
crowd's applause. If they had stayed at home, Gonzalo
would have the crowds at his feet. He would earn as much
respect as Víctor Jara and as much money as Julio Iglesias.
Yet he is becoming famous despite everything. Even living
in a country where nobody can understand his songs will
not hold him back. He was such a childish, uncomplicated
boy when she met him, even simpler than a village girl
like herself; she underestimated his abilities. But he needs
more than his brother's friendship and a bottle in a brown
paper bag. He cannot survive without a family.

—Marta, the man with the paunch and the grey-feath-
ered eyebrows says. —I can't understand you.—

She translates: —Peasants usually walk barefoot and I
am a peasant girl, my love.— She cuts a pirouette through
the grass, dew as sweet as squeezings from a cantaloupe
melon sloshing against her instep. —Ha ha! I speak your
language perfectly. I'm a real Québécoise.—

—The music's stopped, Marta. Why are you still dancing?—

Can't he hear the twang of the guitar, the rippling
chords that shake the canyon night, juddering through
the wall of the shop into the outer room of the house
where she flattens herself against her cot, summoning up
the courage to go and see him play? Can't he hear the
same strong chords, amplified and enhanced, pulsing
through the air of a café on Rue St-Denis next weekend?

—It's starting again, she says.

One of the pudgy boy's friends has slipped a cassette
into the machine; fresh gusts of *música norteamericana* are
billowing from the speakers. She lifts her feet to dance.
He is gesturing at her shoes. Little girls are giggling. *¡Loca!*

¡Loca! If she hadn't escaped the village by marrying
Gonzalo, the children would be pelting her with stones.

—You'll catch cold, he says, his mouth tense.

Don't humiliate me, he means. Does he think she can't
read the desperation in his eyes? She knows him almost
well enough to argue with him like a wife. A few hours
more together and they will never fight free of one another. She feels like a woman leaning farther and farther
out into the muddy river to fill her bucket with water. In
a moment she will lean too far and plunge into Enrique's
torrent, consigning the bucket holding all that she and
Gonzalo share to be washed downstream and out of sight.
She will be immersed in a Québécois life, with no words
to convey to María how her childhood smelled and tasted.

The fat boy has returned to the deck. The microphone
in his hands becomes a glistening trinket. Enrique's relatives bow with laughter like her grandmother genuflecting
in Father Alberto's church. In front of her a little girl trips,
falling to her knees. Juan, Ana and Isabel spin around her
in the swirling dust. She staggers to her feet, groping
towards them. They prance circles around her, laughing
and smiling, until Father Alberto's hoarse roar scares them
away. Mad, tormented man: he snarls because he dreams
of living on the coast and boating among the lianas. She
squats alone on the hard earth, sobbing with pain at her
grazed knee.

—Go down to the river and fill a bucket with water to
cleanse your knee, Marta.—

—Marta! Get up off the grass. We're leaving.—

She gropes towards the riverbank, his heavy palm weigh-
ing against her shoulder. Their hostess's round face fattens
to anchor her rigid smile. Her stretched fingers brush
across Marta's palm. The sound of the river rushing over

big rocks scours the music downstream as they drift out
between the shadows cast by hedges and rooftops standing
beneath the tall streetlights. He guides her towards his car.
The door crunches shut and she is leaving the village for
Quito. Hortensia and the other fruit-sellers wave her a
frantic farewell from beneath the overhang of the control
post. The silent Indian drives the microbus so fast that she
is heaved against the other passengers at every curve.
When Gonzalo tucks his arm around her, she stops trying
to conceal her trembling and pushes her face into the stiff
uniform fabric of his shoulder.

He trails his hand over her hips as he reaches forward
to turn on the radio. Politics spills from the dashboard.

—*Les intérêts du Québec*, . . . Enrique says. —*La langue des
affaires* . . . —

—How can such a rich country waste its time on this
stupid language argument? You have no real problems,
but you make problems for yourselves.—

—Once you have food and clothing, Enrique says, the
next thing you need is culture. Your language is your
culture. And a language you can only speak after five
o'clock in the afternoon is a dead language.—

Nuqa Quitoman risani, she chants inside her head as the
microbus climbs towards the capital in a series of furious
uphill dashes. If she thinks in Quichua her grandmother
will hear her. She will call upon Pachamama, maker of all
things, to preserve her granddaughter in the capital. Her
husband's arm grows leaden, his probing fingers intrusive.

—No, she says, as the streetlights flashing overhead
illumine his thick forearm and the soles of her shoes, still
not returned to her feet, lying between them on the seat.
—I want to go home.—

—Give me directions and I'll drive you to the door.—
His palm descends like a damp mat on her thigh. —Which
way do I go to take you home, Marta?—

—I don't know.—

The racing pattern of streets bewilders her. Broad pla-
zas, enclosed by stately palm trees, shimmer beneath the
percolating arcs of water jetting up from the fountains.
The microbus stops on a sloping square above the market
in the old city. The afternoon turns cold and grey. Sturdy
Indians sway shoulder-to-shoulder down the crowded cobblestoned streets; before he has led her two blocks, she is
lost.

—Drop me at the Jean-Talon Métro station, she says.
—I can walk from there.—

The car twists through back streets. At the top of a steep,
rickety staircase, Gonzalo's father awaits them. —Welcome
to your new family, the wrinkled old man says with re-
hearsed care. From this point on, his hospitality withers;
he ceases to address her directly. Fiercely loyal to his priest,
the old man blames her for converting his son to Evangelical Christianity. He ignores Marta's protestations that
it is Gonzalo who has introduced her to the smiling face
of Jesus Christ. It is he who has made her equal to the city.

The car stops. She barely has time to breathe before he
encloses her in his arms. Their lips press together, then
she feels herself pull back.

She writhes free. —I must go. I must work tomorrow.—

—Please come upstairs.—

—Upstairs?—

She looks and recognizes the balcony and the sign se-
cured to the railing: *NE TOUCHEZ PAS A LA LOI 101.*

—I didn't want to come here. Please take me home. I'm
a *señora decente*, I never wanted . . . —

His torso invades her side of the seat, his hands clutching at her shoulders. —I love you.—

—You can't love me, I'm married!— She pushes at him with her left hand, scrabbling at the doorhandle with her right. The door falls open. She rolls away and thumps down onto hard asphalt.

—Watch out! he shouts.

The last microbus of the evening roars past a few centimetres from her feet.

—Your shoes, Marta!—

—*Pwwaway, Martita. Nuqanchis cieloman risanchis.*—

She delves for the words to reply in Quichua but can only come up with Spanish. —I will fly to you in Heaven, grandmother.—

—I'm sorry, Marta. I didn't mean to frighten you. Come back. I'll drive you home.—

Eluding his hands, she springs to her feet and sprints through the blackness in the direction of the village.

TWENTY FOUR ♪

The spotlights burning through the fog of cigarette smoke concentrate her gaze. The stage stands empty. They sit down at a table at the back of the café. *Une soirée de musique latino-américaine,* the placard at the door announces. The tables at the front have been occupied by long-haired gringos in alpaca sweaters. Clusters of Latino men, smoking and arguing and drinking Belle Gueule and Labatt's Blue, squeeze in around two tables obscured by the trough of shadow below the stage. Touching Alfonsina's arm, Marta says: —The first time I heard Gonzalo play I was too nervous to enter my papi's shop. I stood outside in the darkness and listened to everyone applauding him.—

—You don't have to be nervous now. He needs you, Marta. His reaction in the Métro proves it.— Alfonsina's hinged earrings give an admonishing click.

Marta stares into Alfonsina's impassive, soured face. My friend. Before, she knew only Juana's negligent affection, broken by bouts of hectoring, the fickle sympathy of the women at the control post and the unbearable lessons in matters of dress and cooking that Gonzalo's sisters prescribed for the peasant girl he had brought back from the village. When Alfonsina misunderstands her, the anger that rips through Marta is more ferociously intimate than

the emotions stirred by anyone other than Juana. Even
Gonzalo, in the days after their arrival in Quito, when she
had felt so skimmingly in accord with his sincerity, en-
folded in his music, his strong arms and his rousing dia-
logue with Jesus Christ, could never slash her to the core
with the force of an offhand reproach from Alfonsina.
—Thank you for coming with me tonight.—
    —I'm willing to disappear if you and Gonzalo hit it off.
I can always say I have to get back to the shop. Or when
the Sailor comes, we can say we're going home.—
    —I don't know if we'll hit it off, Marta says, leaning over
the cake-like candle mooring their table. An emaciated,
black-clad waiter, the flick of hair curving over his forehead dyed white-blonde, approaches. Alfonsina orders a
capuccino and, offering to pay, urges Marta to sample this
concoction. Nodding her assent, Marta tries to imagine
feeling attracted to the *payaso* who careered towards her
across the mezzanine of the Jean-Talon Métro station. —I
could never fall for Gonzalo again like I did when I was a
girl. We had nothing to distract us then. It's not like that
anymore. Not with María. Not with rent to pay.— The
waiter presents her with her capuccino. She takes a slurp
at the lip of the mug, giggling as the frothy cream smears
her lips. She wishes she could afford to buy such luxuries
herself. —Back in the village, when I met Gonzalo it was
like magic.—
    —Meeting men was magical when I was a young girl,
too, Alfonsina says. —At home, in Aracataca. Magical and
real at the same time. But when you come to a country
like Canada you must think of practical matters. That's
part of the reason I married the Sailor.—

Marta looks into her friend's eyes, confident her silence will bring forth an explanation more promptly than any question she could ask.

—The Sailor had saved up a *capitalitico* from his years at sea and in the warehouses. He wanted to put the money into a business, but he needed a woman to organize it! We were sleeping together and he liked my empanadas and arepas, so he suggested the shop to me as a business proposition. 'Of course, we'd have to get married,' he said!— Alfonsina's imitation of the Sailor's drawl makes Marta seize Alfonsina's plump forearm in laughter.

—¡*No me cuentas!* Weren't you offended?—

—I was flattered! That shop has made our marriage. Until then, neither of us had a record of staying very long with our lovers. There's always more flesh to savour!—

Marta wishes Alfonsina wouldn't trumpet her savouring of flesh in such a loud voice. The room is crammed with people who understand Spanish. Even the starved-looking boy waiter, hovering to ask if they wish to order again before the music begins, appears stymied by Alfonsina's exuberance. When Alfonsina waves him away, he retreats with offended haste. Marta stares after him, wondering what tales of her friend's lasciviousness he may be spreading. What will people think of them?

The lights dim, veiling Alfonsina's bucktoothed smile with the decency of shadow. A stocky, long-haired man has taken the stage alongside a short, slight woman in a white blouse. He strums the guitar while she sings songs of loss and exile in a Central American accent. During the choruses the man's strumming quickens. The woman, her head darting forward in rhythmic undulations that remind Marta of a chicken foraging in the dirt, belts out upbeat adaptions of dense revolutionary anthems. When the softer music returns her movements grow less convulsive. She shuttles about the stage at her own pace, her eyes fixed on a spot above the audience's heads.

I could walk like that, Marta thinks. The small woman strolling the stage, her voice so much larger than her body, drowns all the tremors of activity scurrying through the café in the strains of her melancholy. Rapt faces lean forward. As the singer hits a high note, Marta gasps: she's turned her suffering into beauty. Is the guitarist her husband? Yet it is the woman's voice that rings out. When my leg recovers . . . She is glad that they didn't sit at the front. Gonzalo, if he is up there in the crowd, would have seen her limping. A week after her flight from Enrique her old limp has returned in painful, hobbling spasms. Fearful of what might happen if she entered the Métro barefoot – could she be arrested for such indecency? – she ran for three blocks after fleeing Enrique's car. It will be weeks before she can match the grace with which the woman in the white blouse ambles to the side of the stage. Her voice dips and subsides, she falls forward in a deep bow. The cigarette haze closes over her for a moment like a blurred shawl, then she swings upright to receive the audience's acclaim. —*¡Qué belleza!* Marta exclaims.

—She's not pretty, Alfonsina says.

—I meant her singing! Marta says.

Before Alfonsina can reply, the Sailor arrives. He kisses his wife on the lips, kisses Marta on both cheeks. Hauling over a chair, he windmills his arm to attract the waiter's attention and orders a Labatt's Blue. His burly weight daunts Marta. He is looking older, though; the sags beneath his mournful eyes have grown deeper, the dim light runs a brownish shadow over his scar.

—So you and Gonzalo are going to be living together again, he says, in a voice she finds uncomfortably loud.

She shakes her head. —I haven't spoken to him. I don't know what he wants.—

The Sailor lowers his elbow onto the table. A lick of wax springs off the candle and congeals on the stained wood. —Tell him that if he doesn't do right by you, he can answer to me. To me and my friends.—

—Yes, Sailor. Thank you so much.—

—I mean that, you know. He's your husband. If he doesn't live up to his martrimonial duties, you let me know.—

—*All* of his matrimonial duties? Alfonsina leers.

The Sailor bellows. Marta bows her head, her cheeks scorching.

The lights go down. —*Mesdames et messieurs*, says the annoucer, *je vous présente Gonzalo Condor et son orchestre chilien!*—

Gonzalo Condor! Marta stares. Yes, this is the man who stumbled after her in the Métro. The same long hair, the same glossy bar of a mustache; the same flamboyant poncho, crowned this time by an Incan earflap hat. Had he once been the shy uniformed boy at the control post, the Gonzalo who carried her away from the village and brought her to Quito and Montreal? Is Rodríguez not a good enough name for a singer?

The name he has scorned belongs to her as well. She is still his wife.

Gonzalo pushes his mouth against the microphone with the confidence she used to hate in him. Marta's anger stands up in her chest. How she longs to put him in his place! She could tell these entranced admirers that the condor on the stage, the wings of his poncho flopping around him, is a modest soldier named Rodríguez who has abandoned his wife and daughter.

She is furious. *¡Me siento tan brava!* I'm so bold I could do anything.

She climbs to her feet.

As soon as she stands she becomes aware that Alfonsina has been scrutinizing her since the moment Gonzalo appeared. The expression on Alfonsina's face mingles surprise with emotions Marta cannot identify. Her large hands clasp in the wavering candlelight.

Marta stands straight, her breast thrust forward. She stares at Gonzalo's earflap hat. And his group is supposed to be Chilean! Not a single haughty, light-skinned Chilean of her acquaintance would be caught dead in an Incan hat. She can barely believe that he is wearing such a garment. At his first glimpse of Montreal in the winter, the gringos transformed into gigantic elves by their tall woollen toques, Gonzalo burst out laughing. He refused to wear the toque she bought for him: —It makes a man look like a *maricón!*— He walked bareheaded through the snow until he began to sneeze.

She feels herself growing taller and straighter. She has never felt so tall. Can he see her? His eyes remain focused above the heads of the audience as he leads the group into a song about building a socialist Chile. When the song ends, he shrugs himself upright and introduces the musicians. Five men in ponchos stand behind him in a broad semi-circle. One plays the drums, one the *rondador*, one the *quena*, one the *charango* and one a guitar like Gonzalo's. All but the second guitarist, a lean mustached man, are wearing ponchos. Gonzalo announces the next song with a call for solidarity, punctuating his bravado by tossing away the earflap cap. He shakes out his hair to its unseemly length. Who does he think he is? How can he *expect* these people to applaud him?

As the music strikes her, she feels stranded in the shadows. Gonzalo is playing in her father's shop. She is marooned in the darkness beyond the lapping light of the doorway, an overwrought girl agonizing over whether to set foot inside. If she hesitates, Hortensia may stumble past, and the whole village will ridicule her.

She steps forward.

Alfonsina and the Sailor are watching her. In their eyes she has become unpredictable. The thought amuses her; she has never felt so sure of herself.

She edges around a table, pushes forward on her aching leg.

—*Franchement!* a voice erupts behind her. —*Laisse-nous voir le show!*—

She continues moving forward. Her eyes chart a path between the tables.

—*Pwwaway, Martita. Nuqanchis . . . nuqanchis. . . .* —

Her grandmother's voice fades. She cannot bring to mind the faces of Juan, Ana and Isabel. Her surroundings consume her: she notices the Export A logo embossed on the white plastic ashtray in the middle of the table she is easing past, the harsh smell of cigarette ash mingling with the more pungent odour of the lighted cigarette being smoked by the man seated at her elbow, the curl of the collar of the jacket slung over the back of the chair brushing her hip, the alternation of patches of glare and shadow spotting her progress towards the stage. She walks down a vibrating corridor of music, startled by the force and strength of Gonzalo's playing. Impervious to his fetching smiles and impassioned appeals for solidarity, she still weakens before his wild, solemn charisma. His chords tumble through her chest. Gonzalo has changed. The gestures so practised, the smiles so deftly coordinated; the man on the stage is chilly and calculating. She feels it when she looks up, seeking out his eyes. Gonzalo's days of bad jobs and heavy drinking may be nearing an end, but he has killed the boy from the control post.

She steps into the gap below the stage, nearly tripping on thick cables. The waiter starts forward, anxiety sharpening his features. He touches her shoulder. —*Excusez-moi, Madame . . .* —

—*Fais-toi-z-en-pas*, she tells him in her best Québécois. —I don't want to bother them. I just want to see them close up.—

The boy hesitates. Her husband's groomed husk cavorts above her. His blow-dried locks glisten. She cannot imagine how much he must have paid for the white shirt with the embroidered collar that he is wearing beneath his poncho. She stares up, the waiter lingering at her elbow, until Gonzalo looks down. Surprise dashes through his eyes. But it is only a quiver; his smile remains in place. When he glances down again his expression has solidified.

—*Señora, ¿quiere sentarse?*— The whisper reaches her in the ruffled moment between the end of the song and the beginning of the applause. One of the men at the table closest to the stage has vacated his seat for her. Grateful, she sits down. The waiter scoots away. The men nod their greetings. On the stage Gonzalo announces that this is their last song of the evening, but next year they will be releasing their first CD. Scattered whoops. Gonzalo smiles that brilliant, false smile of which she has absolutely no memory. The last song is about a snail, the snail of revolution, refusing to be turned back by any obstacle, edging ever closer to victory. Marta wishes she could fall in love

with his music. His guitar-playing impresses her yet does
not move her.

But that is only part of the reason she cannot go back
to him.

As soon as his set is over, heralded by thudding, stamping applause, he locks his guitar in its case at the side of
the stage. Before Marta can think about returning to Alfonsina's side, Gonzalo hops down in front of her. She
stands to greet him. As he clasps her, kissing her on both
cheeks, then, fleetingly, on the lips, she thinks: he's heavier than he used to be, but he's only a hair taller than me.
Next to Enrique, I was a dwarf . . .

—*¡Marta! ¡Mi amorcita!* I'm so happy to see you! . . . —
Yes, this is the man from the Métro. In the absence of an
audience – or is it in the presence of his estranged wife?
– his eyes lose their gleam. His need flows towards her
undiluted, no matter how hard he tries to hide it. She can
see that the men at the table, regarding them with indul-
gent smiles, are taken in by his arrogance. Marta feels
depressed: it will always be like this between them, the
problems will never change. —You don't know how I miss
you, *mi amor*! I've been wanting to see you so badly . . . —

—You knew where to find me. I'm still in that room
you've stopped helping to pay for. With your daughter.—

Gonzalo shoots a glance at the men at the table. A
couple of them stare back at him, but the others turn away
to compete for the attention of the waiter. Gonzalo pulls
on her forearm; they stumble towards the spotlights. The
foot of her bad leg pivoting on a cable, she hoists herself
up onto the lip of the stage.

—Martita, he says, pushing his face close to hers. —I'll
make it up to you! Everything will be better this time. You
can see how well it's going. I'm not making much money

yet, but in a few months . . . We'll buy a condo with a view of the Mountain. I promise you! You don't know how I've missed you. All I want is for us to be together again as a family . . . —

His palms paw at her hips. She feels cold and uncomfortable. She grips his wrists to remove his hands, but he resists. They wrestle for a moment and she nearly topples back onto the stage, where two men are arranging a drum set for the next act. As her head swings back, a hot spotlight glares into her eyes. —Gonzalo, everybody can see us!—

—*Mi amorcita* . . . —

He relaxes his grip. She straightens up, sitting on the front of the stage, and stares out at the twittering audience. Alfonsina and the Sailor have dissolved into the fog of cigarette smoke. All these people staring at her. In the village she had never met so many people. She would have been ashamed to speak of family matters, even in a lowered voice, in a public place. She would have been ashamed to show her face. —Gonzalo, she says, no longer caring whether the men at the front table can overhear them, I'm not going to live with you again.—

—But Marta . . .— His groping eyes turn savage, his hands pinch her shoulders: —There's another man! *Claro.* Who is he? Some rich gringo bastard! . . . —

—There's no other man. But the Ochoas want me to leave. I can't afford an apartment on my own. Not with María; it's too expensive. I want you to pay me enough every month so that María and I can afford our own apartment. I'm still working; that's not going to stop. But a woman doesn't get paid as much as a man. You have a responsibility to me and a big responsibility to your daughter.—

—Martita! Don't be like that . . . —

—This is how I am. Just as that's how you are!— She flicks the corner of his poncho.

He twists away. —You think I'm rich . . . —

—That doesn't interest me. I just expect you to be responsible.—

—Why should I pay for you? You've got some gringo . . . You're swindling me!—

—Is everything all right here? the Sailor says in his sleepy drawl. Gonzalo shrinks between the height and bulk of Alfonsina and her husband. Marta, riding above him on her spar of stage, stares down into his eyes.

—She doesn't understand, Gonzalo mumbles.

—What I don't understand is how any man can be so *bruto* as to let his daughter grow up hungry just because he likes having a drink.—

Gonzalo's silence sinks beneath the hurried clumping sounds of the stage being cleared for the next act.

—An *hombre* has his responsibilities, no? the Sailor says, giving Gonzalo a comradely punch in the shoulder. Gonzalo says nothing. The Sailor punches him again, in exactly the same spot, twice as hard as before. Gonzalo starts back, floundering against Alfonsina's ample breast. —Other men don't respect a guy who doesn't fulfill his obligations, the Sailor says. —Not my buddies, anyway. My buddies from the port and the warehouse. They treat guys like that pretty badly. Especially if they know a man's starting to make money.—

—Maybe I could pay a hundred dollars a month, Gonzalo mutters.

—Two hundred! Marta says. —That's the least you can do.—

—*Asseyez-vous, s'il vous plaît,* the announcer says. Walking to the front of the stage, he cups his hand over the head of the microphone as he leans over them. —*Le show recommence!—*

Marta slides down off the stage. A jab of pain shimmers up her bad leg. The Sailor lays his arm on Gonzalo's shoulder. —Come sit with us for a while.—

They work their way towards the back of the café. As they sit down at the table where Marta's, Alfonsina's and the Sailor's jackets remain draped over the backs of their chairs, Alfonsina says: —So the question my husband asked you was: is everything all right?—

Marta looks at Gonzalo pulling up a chair opposite her. He deals her a surly, bruised glance, then turns away. She stares at him, scouring out the boy soldier's face behind the hair, mustache and glossy new flesh. His gaze lifts, meeting her eyes in a kind of desolation; his body shifting into a more upright posture, he gives a despairing shrug of his shoulders.

Turning to Alfonsina, Marta says: —I think we're starting to get somewhere.—

¶

Sitting in the grey light of the front room, Marta watches her daughter lope up the lawn. Her shiny gold slacks accentuate her long-legged spryness. Her loose kinky dark hair slides on her shoulders. She enters the house humming a tune, her face blank with candour yet composed beneath her make-up.

Marta feels her body trembling in fury. —*¡Carajo!* she says, crossing the room. She seizes María by the arm. —Where the hell have you been, *atrevida?*—

—I slept with Jean-Louis, María says in French.

Her sullenness lasts only an instant. Her mood shifting, she shrugs away the tension between them. Marta drops her daughter's arm. She feels emptied of words, anger, authority.

María stares down into her face. Neither of them speaks. María flings her arms around Marta in a breath-sucking hug. —*Pauvre Maman!* Nothing new is going to happen to you again.—

/

Printed in March 1998 by

ON DEMAND PRINTING INC.

in Boucherville, Quebec